BRONTË FACTS AND BRONTË PROBLEMS

BRONTË FACTS AND BRONTË PROBLEMS

Edward Chitham and Tom Winnifrith

First published 1983 by
THE MACMILLAN PRESS LTD
London and Basingstoke
Companies and representatives
throughout the world

ISBN 0 333 30698 8

Filmsetting by
Vantage Photosetting Co. Ltd
Eastleigh and London
Printed in Hong Kong

To all our students of the Brontës

Contents

Acknowledgements

The authors should like to thank Mrs Lily Fry, Miss Elizabeth Greenwood, Miss Ann Griffin and Mrs Christine Wyman for their help in typing, and Miss Karla Bohn for producing the magnificent final copy. They should also like to thank Mrs Julia Steward and Miss Valery Brooks of Macmillan for producing the final version so promptly and efficiently.

Dr Winnifrith must acknowledge the financial support of the British Academy and the University of Warwick, which enabled him to visit libraries in America. He acknowledges help from these libraries, notably the Special Collections Centre at the University of Vancouver, British Columbia, the Humanities Research Centre at the University of Texas, and the Henry W. and Albert A. Berg Collection, the New York Public Library, Astor, Lenox and Tilden Foundations. Both authors must thank the Brontë Society, Haworth, and their indefatigable librarian, Mrs Sally Stonehouse. Mr Chitham should like to express his thanks also to Mr Charles Lemon, editor of *Brontë Society Transactions*, in whose publication earlier versions of the ideas on Shelley and on the literary relationship between Emily and Anne Brontë first appeared. He should also like to thank authorities at the Polytechnic, Wolverhampton, for allocation of time to enable the work to be undertaken.

Each author is entirely responsible for the chapters under his name, although we have read each other's work.

List of Abbreviations

BPM   The Brontë Parsonage Museum

BST   *Brontë Society Transactions*

H   C. W. Hatfield (ed.), *The Complete Poems of Emily Jane Brontë* (Oxford, 1941)

MLR   *Modern Language Review*

SHBL   T. J. Wise and J. A. Symington (eds), *The Brontës: Their Lives, Friendships and Correspondence*, 4 vols (Oxford, 1932)

SHCBP   T. J. Wise and J. A. Symington (eds), *The Complete Poems of Charlotte and Patrick Branwell Brontë* (Oxford, 1934)

Introduction

TOM WINNIFRITH

Books and articles on the Brontës continue to emerge at an alarming rate, and we begin unpromisingly with an apology for adding to their number. Perhaps our uncompromisingly dreary title will discourage readers from thinking that we are either adding to the list of books with titles like *Purple Heather* which aim to tell the same old moving Brontë story in a new and original way, or adding to the list of articles with titles like 'Heathcliff and the Analogy of Self Revelation' which aim by subtle examination of the Brontës' imagery to shed fresh light upon their novels. Without wishing to be too disparaging to recent work on the Brontës, of which there is an excellent account by H. J. Rosengarten in *Victorian Fiction* (ed. G. Ford, New York, 1978), we do both feel that much of the biographical and critical effort of the past few years has been misdirected. The biographical work has been marred by too ready acceptance of secondary sources, unreliable evidence and shaky chronology: it has also accepted too naïvely a simple equation between people and places in the Brontës' lives and people and places in their books. The critical articles have shied away from biography altogether, perhaps put off by the *naïveté* of the biographers or the complexity of the biographical information or the feeling that biography and criticism do not mix. And yet, as certain chapters in this book set out to prove, the Brontës' lives are important for a study of their works, although it is necessary to see them steadily and to see them whole.

The first necessity for a complete understanding of the Brontës is an adequate supply of reliable texts, and these we simply do not have. Much of the work in this book has arisen from our labours in editing the poetry of the Brontës. Mr Chitham has already edited Anne Brontë's poetry for Macmillan (London, 1979) and is in the process of editing Emily's poetry for the Oxford University Press in collaboration with Derek Roper. I am editing Charlotte's and Branwell's poetry for

Blackwell, revising the Shakespeare Head volume, edited by the infamous T. J. Wise and J. A. Symington. In the second chapter, 'Texts and Transmission', I have endeavoured to throw fresh light on just why and how the Shakespeare Head came to be edited so badly, while at the same time paying due tribute to the one man, C. W. Hatfield, who ensured that some sort of rescue operation on the Brontës' poetry can still be mounted.

Poetry is, of course, a dangerous medium on which to mount biographical or literary speculation, although I attempt this rather rashly in the opening chapter. Mr Chitham's main purpose in writing on Emily's poetry is an interpretative one. He points out the dangers of trying to fit all Emily's poetry into a straitjacket, whether it be Gondal, biographical or philosophical, although clearly these factors have to be taken into account when considering Emily as a poet. Emily, as easily the greatest of the four Brontës, naturally receives the greatest amount of critical attention, and the chapters on Anne's and Branwell's poetry have important lessons for students of Emily, although Anne and Branwell are not bad poets in their own right. Charlotte put her poetry into her prose, and it is as providing an insight into both her novels and her life that we print the first unpublished poem.

Mr Chitham's first essay in Chapter 3 is designed to establish the chronology of the Brontës' early years. It may be asked why it is important that we are certain about the chronology of the period some ten years before the publication of the novels. Many conclusions have been rashly drawn from too ready an acceptance of the standard dating in biographies which are themselves dependent upon guesswork, hypotheses and the dubious dates of Mrs Gaskell, Ellen Nussey or C. K. Shorter. Charlotte has been accused of being unfair to Emily's memory, and Emily of being totally unable to survive outside her home. Mr Chitham's aim is to set Emily's poetry firmly in a factual context, thus shattering much shallow speculation.

The fourth and fifth chapters on Emily's poetic inspiration and Gondal's Queen do not, as Mr Chitham points out, say all that much about Emily's greatest poems. Instead, by clearing away much of the lumber involved in previous analyses of Emily as a mystic poet and as a poet of Gondal, Mr Chitham opens the way for such investigations of Emily's genius as he himself attempts in his final chapter. Gondal has been seen by some, notably Miss Fannie Ratchford, as the key to a proper understanding of Emily's poetry, but to too many it has acted as a barrier, and if we have not removed this barrier at least we have tried to bypass it.

Before his final chapter on Emily's vision Mr Chitham examines the vexed question of the relationship between Emily and other poets, and between Emily and Anne. In the later essay he is following previous work in 'Almost like Twins' in *BST* and his edition of Anne Brontë's poetry. Similarly, I am following previous ideas first suggested in my two books on the Brontës when I discuss possible sources for Branwell's poetry in the library at Ponden Hall and when I consider the composition of *Wuthering Heights.*

In these four chapters, though the focus may seem to be on one particular Brontë, we are really considering the Brontës as a whole, though bearing in mind that the closeness of the Brontës to each other brought certain strains within the family. The focus may seem to switch to and fro between biography and literary history, but its principal purpose is ultimately critical, the evaluation of the Brontës' poetry and of *Wuthering Heights.* The similarities between the Brontës and previous poets, between one Brontë and another, and between a possible one volume *Wuthering Heights* and the present novel are critically less interesting than the differences.

In the final chapter I return to biography and to Charlotte Brontë, although the most interesting remarks in Ellen Nussey's unpublished manuscript for and letters to Wemyss Reid concern Emily Brontë, Mr Brontë and Ellen herself. Ellen's account of the Brontës, though clearly a discovery, cannot be reckoned to be a revelation of the same order as Spielmann's publication of the Heger letters, which casts a wholly new light upon Charlotte Brontë and upon her novels with schoolmasters or Belgians or married men or a combination of these acting as heroes. Interest in the Brontës' biography was quickened by such discoveries, and research students may still hope to find gold by scrabbling under the fast vanishing cobblestones of Brussels, although perhaps they would do better to direct their attention to the Berg Collection in New York.

Ellen Nussey does not appear in a very attractive light in her correspondence with Wemyss Reid, and it is salutary for biographers to realise just how much information about the unconventional Charlotte is dependent upon the prim Ellen. Ellen almost certainly did not know about Charlotte's love for M. Heger, and her pious wish to preserve her friend's memory from all accusations of immorality must involve a considerable distortion of the truth. There is a warning here for both biographers and literary critics who rely on biography. What such biographers and critics need is a proper edition of Charlotte's letters, although since even this edition will be dominated by correspondence to Ellen Nussey it is unlikely that we will ever get anything but a rather one-sided portrait of the Brontës.

In this book we have tried to see the Brontës from many angles, considering poetry as well as prose, biography as well as criticism, Branwell and Anne as well as Emily and Charlotte. At the same time, we have not set out to give a complete picture of the Brontës, believing indeed that it is a fault of many books on the Brontës that they try and set out all the facts without seeing all the problems, just as it is a fault of many articles that they try and see all the Brontë story in the light of one particular problem. One important area that we have only touched upon is the juvenilia. This is mainly because the prose juvenilia have not yet been edited properly, although the forthcoming editions of Charlotte's juvenilia by Dr Christine Alexander, to be published by Blackwell, will bring to light many new facts and clear up a few problems. One problem a new edition of the juvenilia will solve is the question of just how good these early unpublished prose stories by Charlotte are; some of the claims made for them are certainly exaggerated.

In spite of our prosaic title we do not wish to minimise the poetic charm and appeal of the Brontës' books and their lives, nor to discourage people from seeking to trace links between the two. But for a variety of reasons this is a much harder task than most readers imagine, and we will have succeeded if we have shown some of the difficulties that still stand in the way of proper academic study of the Brontës.

1 Charlotte Brontë and Mr Rochester

TOM WINNIFRITH

A.
       At first I did attention give,
       Observance – deep esteem;
       His frown I failed not to forgive,
       His smile – a boon to deem.

       Attention rose to interest soon,
       Respect to homage changed;
       The smile became a *relived* [?] boon,
       The frown like grief estranged.

       The interest ceased not with his voice,
       The homage *tracked* [?] him near.
                 ~~his tread~~
       Obedience was my heart's free choice –
       Whate'er his mood severe [?].

       His praise infrequent – favour rare,
       Unruly deceivers [?] grew.
       And too much power a haunting fear
       Around his anger threw.

       His coming was my hope each day,
       His parting was my pain
                 ~~grief~~
       The chance that did his steps delay
       Was ice in every vein.

1

I gave entire affection now,
I gave devotion sure,
~~deep~~
And strong took root and fast did grow
One mighty feeling more.

The truest love that ever heart
Felt at its kindled core
Through my veins with quickened start
~~Then did the veil of doubt depart~~
A tide of life did pour.
~~And life a glory wore.~~

[A] halo played about the brows
~~It played~~   ~~the awful brow~~
of life as seen by me,
And *trailing* [?] bliss within me rose,
And anxious ecstacy.

I dreamed it would be nameless bliss
As I loved loved to be,
And to this object did I press
As blind as eagerly.

But wild and pathless was the space
~~And~~
That lay our lives between,
And dangerous as the foaming race
of ocean's surges green,
                    ~~brilliant~~

And haunted as a robber path
                    ~~barren track~~
Through wilderness or wood,
For might and right, woe and wrath
        ~~hate and love, delight and wrath~~
Between our spirits stood.

I dangers dared, I hindrance scorned
I omens did defy;
    ~~feelings~~
Whatever menaced, harassed, warned
I passed impetuous by.

On sped my rainbow fast as light,
I flew as in a dream,
For glorious rose upon my sight
That child of shower and gleam,

And bright on clouds of suffering dim
Shone that soft solemn joy.
I care not then how dense and grim
Disasters gather nigh
        [?] ~~brings nigh~~

I care not in this moment sweet,
The hate, the love, the joy, the sweet

Though all I have rushed oer
The wrath I had passed over

Should come on pinion strong and fleet
These came

Proclaiming vengeance sore.

Hate struck me in his presence down,
Love barred approach to me,
My rival's joy with jealous frown
Declared hostility.

Wrath leagued with calumny transfused
Strong poison in his veins
            ~~soul~~
And I stood at his feet accused
Of false – strains

Cold as a statue's grew his eye,
Hard as a rock his brow,
Cold hard to me – but tenderly
He kissed my rival now.

She seemed my rainbow to have seized,
~~reached~~
Around her form it closed,
And soft its iris splendour blazed
Where love and she reposed.

B.   The truest love that ever heart
    Felt at its kindled core
Did through each vein, in quickened start,
    The tide of being pour.

Her coming was my hope each day,
    Her parting was my pain;
The chance that did her steps delay
    Was ice in every vein.

I dreamed it would be nameless bliss,
    As I loved, loved to be;
And to this object did I press
    As blind as eagerly.

But wide as pathless was the space
    That lay, our lives, between,
And dangerous as the foamy race
    Of ocean-surges green.

And haunted as a robber-path
    Through wilderness or wood;
For Might and Right, and Woe and Wrath,
    Between our spirits stood.

I dangers dared; I hind'rance scorned;
    I omens did defy:
Whatever menaced, harassed, warned,
    I passed impetuous by.

On sped my rainbow, fast as light;
    I flew as in a dream;
For glorious rose upon my sight
    That child of Shower and Gleam.

Still bright on clouds of suffering dim
　　Shines that soft, solemn joy;
Nor care I now, how dense and grim
　　Disasters gather nigh.

I care not in this moment sweet,
　　Though all I have rushed o'er
Should come on pinion, strong and fleet,
　　Proclaiming vengeance sore:

Though haughty Hate should strike me down,
　　Right, bar approach to me,
And grinding Might, with furious frown,
　　Swear endless enmity.

My love has placed her little hand
　　With noble faith in mine,
And vowed that wedlock's sacred band
　　Our nature shall entwine.

My love has sworn, with sealing kiss,
　　With me to live – to die;
I have at last my nameless bliss:
　　As I love – loved am I!

C.　　　　I gave, at first, attention close;
　　　　　Then interest warm ensued;
　　　　From interest, as improvement rose
　　　　　Succeeded gratitude.

　　　　Obedience was no effort soon,
　　　　　And labour was no pain;
　　　　If tired, a word, a glance alone
　　　　　Would give me strength again.

　　　　From others of the studious band,
　　　　　Ere long he singled me;
　　　　But only by more close demand,
　　　　　And sterner urgency.

The task he from another took,
    From me he did reject;
He would no slight omission brook,
    And suffer no defect.

If my companions went astray,
    He scarce their wanderings blam'd;
If I but falter'd in the way,
    His anger fiercely flam'd.

When sickness stay'd awhile my course,
    He seem'd impatient still,
Because his pupil's flagging force
    Could not obey his will.

One day when summoned to the bed
    Where pain and I did strive,
I heard him, as he bent his head,
    Say, 'God, she *must* revive!'

I felt his hand, with gentle stress,
    A moment laid on mine,
And wished to mark my consciousness
    By some responsive sign.

But pow'rless then to speak or move,
    I only felt, within,
The sense of Hope, the strength of Love,
    Their healing work begin.

And as he from the room withdrew,
    My heart his steps pursued;
I long'd to prove, by efforts new,
    My speechless gratitude.

When once again I took my place,
    Long vacant, in the class,
Th' unfrequent smile across his face
    Did for one moment pass.

The lessons done; the signal made
  Of glad release and play.
He, as he passed, an instant stay'd,
  One kindly word to say.

'Jane, till to-morrow you are free
  From tedious task and rule;
This afternoon I must not see
  That yet pale face in school.

'Seek in the garden-shades a seat,
  Far from the play-ground din;
The sun is warm, the air is sweet:
  Stay till I call you in.'

A long and pleasant afternoon
  I passed in those green bowers;
All silent, tranquil, and alone
  With birds, and bees, and flowers.

Yet, when my master's voice I heard
  Call, from the window, 'Jane!'
I entered, joyful, at the word,
  The busy house again.

He, in the hall, paced up and down;
  He paused as I passed by;
His forehead stern relaxed its frown:
  He raised his deep-set eye.

'Not quite so pale,' he murmured low.
  'Now, Jane, go rest awhile.'
And as I smiled, his smoothened brow
  Returned as glad a smile.

My perfect health restored, he took
  His mien austere again;
And, as before, he would not brook
  The slightest fault from Jane.

The longest task, the hardest theme
    Fell to my share as erst,
And still I toiled to place my name
    In every study first.

He yet begrudged and stinted praise,
    But I had learnt to read
The secret meaning of his face,
    And that was my best meed.

Even when his hasty temper spoke
    In tones that sorrow stirred,
My grief was lulled as soon as woke
    By some relenting word

And when he lent some precious book,
    Or gave some fragrant flower,
I did not quail to Envy's look,
    Upheld by Pleasure's power.

At last our school ranks took their ground;
    The hard-fought field I won;
The prize, a laurel wreath, was bound
    My throbbing forehead on.

Low at my master's knee I bent,
    The offered crown to meet;
Its green leaves through my temples sent
    A thrill as wild as sweet.

The strong pulse of Ambition struck
    In every vein I owned;
At the same instant, bleeding broke
    A secret, inward wound.

The hour of triumph was to me
    The hour of sorrow sore;
A day hence I must cross the sea,
    Ne'er to recross it more.

An hour hence, in my master's room,
    I with him sat alone,
And told him what a dreary gloom
    O'er joy had parting thrown.

He little said; the time was brief,
    The ship was soon to sail.
And while I sobbed in bitter grief,
    My master but looked pale.

They called in haste; he bade me go,
    Then snatched me back again;
He held me fast and murmured low,
    'Why will they part us, Jane?

'Were you not happy in my care?
    Did I not faithful prove?
Will others to my darling bear
    As true, as deep a love?

'O God, watch o'er my foster child!
    O guard her gentle head!
When winds are high and tempests wild
    Protection round her spread!

'They call again; leave then my breast;
    Quit thy true shelter, Jane;
But when deceived, repulsed, opprest,
    Come home to me again!'

In the Berg Collection in New York Public Library there is a manuscript, hitherto unpublished in full, which could shed an interesting light on Charlotte Brontë's life and works.[1] The handwriting is Charlotte's normal hand, but it is extremely difficult to read, as she has written in pencil with many crossings out. Nor is it possible to date the manuscript with any accuracy although it must, as will be shown, precede the composition of *Jane Eyre*. Also in the Berg Collection there is the manuscript of a poem, on the back of which there is a letter to W. S. Williams, dated 13 December 1847. This poem, 'He saw my heart's woe,/discovered [actually the manuscript reads discerned] my heart's anguish', is similarly written in pencil, and appears to have the same autobiographical theme. But it is by no means certain that either poem can be dated to 1847.

One interesting feature of the hitherto unpublished poem (A) is the close relation it bears to two of the poems which appear in two of Charlotte's novels. Frances Henri, the shy pupil in *The Professor* is made in Chapter 23 to write a rather feeble poem, beginning 'I gave, at first, attention close, then interest warm ensued' (C). There is a rough draft of this poem at Haworth with many crossings out, differing slightly from the final manuscript version which is in the Pierpont Morgan Library. The poem in *The Professor* tells us of how a pupil fell in love with her teacher, who originally neglected her, but then acknowledged his love, although they were soon to separate, as she had to sail overseas. The manuscript is contained in a notebook headed 'Bruxelles 1843', and the situation must remind us of M. Heger and Charlotte and of M. Paul Emanuel and Lucy Snowe as well as of William Crimsworth and Frances Henri. The pupil is called Jane, but her love seems to be very proper.

The manuscript in the Berg Collection appears to begin in very much the same vein with the words 'At first I did attention give,/observance – deep esteem' and there is the same note of respect turning to love on the part of the pupil in spite of seeming indifference on the part of the teacher. But then a wilder note is struck. The love becomes passionate, unrestrained and doomed because it is unlawful. And the fifth, seventh and ninth to fifteenth stanzas appear with a few corrections in *Jane Eyre* (B) as Rochester's song to Jane, although the fifth has the sex of the loved one changed and appears as the second stanza in *Jane Eyre*.

The omitted sixth and eighth stanzas do not add much to the poem, but the final four stanzas are very different from the printed version in *Jane Eyre*, where in spite of the grim disasters gathering nigh Rochester is consoled by the thought that, though haughty Hate should strike him down, his love has placed her little hand in his. This contrasts with the Berg version where Hate does strike down the heroine, and her lover transfers his affection to a rival.

That the Berg manuscript precedes *Jane Eyre* is shown fairly clearly by the corrections Charlotte has made to the Berg poem with Charlotte altering her first version on many occasions to give the same reading as the poem in *Jane Eyre*. Nor can we contemplate any reason why after 1847 Charlotte should take the poem she had already printed, and scribble an alternative version of it with the changed ending and the significant change of sex. It is therefore certain that at some time before 1847 when George Smith read *Jane Eyre* in manuscript Charlotte wrote the Berg poem, and later adapted it for inclusion in *Jane Eyre*.

I have previously poured scorn on those who have sought to draw parallels between the lives of the Brontës and their works, and upon those who have sought to draw conclusions about the novels from a study of the Brontës' juvenilia and poetry. The Berg manuscript as it stands makes this scorn a little premature. The story it recounts is not the story of any Brontë heroine. Frances Henri's respect turns to love, and she fears a rival who opposes this love in the shape of Mlle Reuter, but the rival does not prevail, and in no sense is the love lawless. Nor for that matter is the love of two other pupils for their teachers, the love of Shirley for Louis Moore, and Lucy Snowe for Paul Emanuel, although as the Berg manuscript predates *Jane Eyre* the poem cannot refer to *Shirley* or *Villette*. Unlike the poem in *The Professor* the Berg manuscript does not refer specifically to a love affair between a pupil and a teacher, and could apply equally well to a governess and her employer, but it is part of Jane Eyre's charm that she is not especially obedient or respectful to Rochester, nor of course, though her love is lawless, does she know that it is, and therefore the sentiments of the narrator of the Berg poem are not those of Jane Eyre.

Rochester does of course know that his love is sinful, and given the necessary change in sex in the fifth stanza the verses are clearly in part suitable to Rochester. But the first part, stressing the lover's respectful obedience and the last part stressing the rival are totally inappropriate to Rochester, and the poem, though in part suitable to adaptation for Rochester's love for Jane, cannot have been written with Rochester in mind.

Zamorna's many loves are not all sanctioned by the marriage tie, and some of his lovers, notably Mina Laury, are in a suitably subordinate position to make the Berg poem suitable in part for them. But the Berg poem would seem to date to the period between 1843 and 1847, by which time Charlotte had abandoned Angria. It is not written in minuscule handwriting, nor in the amoral words of Angria do we find the consciousness of sin which is a feature of the Berg poem.

There is however one story which fits every part of the Berg poem, and this is the story of Charlotte's love for M. Heger. She respected him in spite or because of his sternness, and then grew to love him, hoping his love would be returned, although she knew it was unlawful. Instead there was opposition and calumny. M. Heger grew stern and distant, and Charlotte had the mortification of seeing him love Mme Heger. This is clearly what happened in Belgium, although this was not acknowledged until the discovery of Charlotte's letters to M. Heger. Even these letters, and we clearly do not have them all, express Charlotte's love rather less passionately than the Berg poem. The two generations of Victorian biographers who refused to countenance any love affair have made their mark, and even today the intensity of Charlotte's passion is discussed in fairly respectful tones. In this sense the Berg poem is probably a better guide to Charlotte's feelings than either the prim letters and the biographies based upon them, or the novels, where the hated rival is not really an obstacle, as she is either not married to the hero, or, if married, conveniently dies.

So much for biography. Critically the Berg poem is even more interesting. The timid Frances Henri and the swashbuckling Mr Rochester do not appear to have much in common, and yet they are linked by the feelings of Charlotte Brontë herself. It is generally recognised that one of the reasons for *The Professor*'s failure is that, perhaps anxious to throw a smokescreen over her feelings for M. Heger, Charlotte disguised herself as the male narrator, Crimsworth. As a result we see Frances Henri only through Crimsworth's eyes, and she seems therefore dull and pathetic, while Crimsworth himself alternates between doggish sensuality and tepid affection in a very awkward fashion. Nevertheless we do feel the two characters suit each other, and this is not surprising since they are both reflections of Charlotte herself, although not the real passionate Charlotte.

What is not usually acknowledged is that there is the same similarity between the passionate Jane Eyre and the passionate Rochester, both of whom have to learn to temper their passion. Rochester is, like Crimsworth, a slightly preposterous figure with his masculine masterful ways and merry chat about his mistresses, but it is one of the odd things about *Jane Eyre* that even male readers have a soft spot for Rochester, in spite of the caddish way he behaves. It is right that Jane should marry Rochester whose passionate nature matches her own; how wrong it would be if she had let her fierce flame be crushed by the cold marble of St. John Rivers. Rochester is sympathetic to Jane and sympathetic to us because he is part of Charlotte Brontë. Unlike Jane Eyre who had seen nothing wrong, though all was rather surprising, in her courtship, and unlike M. Heger, against whom no charge can be laid except the mild one of encouraging his promising plain pupils, Mr Rochester certainly and Charlotte Brontë probably on the evidence of the Berg manuscript contemplated adultery. We do not admire

Rochester for this, but we can sympathise with him in the knowledge that his creator was able to transmute her adulterous thoughts into great art.

NOTE

1. I am grateful to the Henry W. and Albert A. Berg Collection, the New York Public Library, Astor, Lenox and Tilden Foundations, for permission to print for the first time the poem with which this chapter begins, and to Professor Victor Neufeldt for helping me with many difficult readings which he had established in preparing his forthcoming edition of Charlotte Brontë's poems.

2 Texts and Transmission

TOM WINNIFRITH

The Brontës have been both lucky and unlucky in their editors. The sympathetic, honourable and efficient George Smith contrasts with the mercenary and incompetent T. H. Newby. Good novelists like Mrs Gaskell and Mrs Humphry Ward saw the greatness of the Brontë sisters in spite of their faults, but their modern successors have been unable to distinguish between sense and sentimentality. The novels are now being properly edited in a scholarly edition. Editing the letters, the poetry and the juvenilia is a harder task. This is because the manuscripts came into the hands of a series of editors who were as unscrupulous as they were inefficient. The task would indeed be quite impossible had it not been for the labours of one man, C. W. Hatfield, who apart from his edition of Emily's poetry, is virtually unknown in Brontë circles.

The unscrupulous editors were C. K. Shorter and T. J. Wise. I have written elsewhere of the villainy of both Shorter and Wise in first acquiring and then disposing of both Charlotte's letters to Ellen Nussey and the collection of juvenilia and poetry which Mr Nicholls had kept in Ireland. In *The Brontës and their Background* I hinted that Wise might even have resorted to passing off as Charlotte's manuscripts that were wholly or partly written by Branwell. An examination of the manuscripts in America suggests that this particular accusation is unjustified. Charlotte did stitch her manuscripts together, and they have not been as widely scattered as Branwell's. Her handwriting is distinct from that of Branwell who conveniently does not cross his ts, and what seems at first a suspicious multiplicity of signatures is indeed a rather endearing form of identification by Charlotte of every piece she wrote. There was some confusion at one stage between poems of Emily and poems of Branwell, but this has been cleared up through the labours of Hatfield.

In the Special Collections, the Library, University of Columbia, Item no. 186 of the Thomas Wise Collection acquired from Mr W. A.

Stockett, there are 66 letters from Hatfield to Davidson Cook. These letters written between 1921 and 1928 are invaluable insights into the difficulties created by Wise and Shorter, and Hatfield's Herculean efforts to clear them up. Hatfield is not particularly unkind to Wise, who had yet to be exposed as a forger, although he does say in a letter dated 9 January 1926 that he could say a great deal about the sacrilegious way in which the manuscripts had been treated. Shorter is described as remarkably careless in the same letter. In a letter of 10 December 1925 we learn that the Hodder & Stoughton editions of the poems of Emily, Charlotte and Anne Brontë were in fact the work of Hatfield, who gained no penny from the work he had done. Shorter, he says, in a letter of 29 October lost the first copy of the Charlotte poems, and very nearly did the same with Branwell's poems which Hatfield had copied out. These were discovered after Shorter's death in the hands of T. J. Wise, who was to make them the basis of his Shakespeare Head edition of Charlotte's and Branwell's poetry.[1]

The Hodder & Stoughton editions of the poems are not satisfactory, being far inferior to the 1941 Oxford edition by Hatfield and the modern edition of Anne's poems by E. Chitham. But in his correspondence to Davidson Cook Hatfield makes it clear why they are unsatisfactory. Very often he was relying not on the original manuscript, but on transcripts made by some minions of Shorter and Wise. He describes these transcripts on 10 December 1925 as made some thirty years before, and on 9 January 1926 said they were by a half-dozen different hands. Shorter again and again is shown not to care about the manuscripts, being ready to accept any printed version. Thus on 28 June 1928 Hatfield complained that he had asked Shorter for the manuscript of *The Violet* by Charlotte Brontë, but was only sent the printed version. On 12 January 1926 Shorter is said to have preferred the inaccurate American edition of Dodd Noble to his own transcripts. On 7 June 1927 there comes the damning indictment that Shorter had known of the existence of both the Honresfeld manuscript of Emily's poems, now vanished, and the Murray manuscript, now in the British Museum, but had not bothered to inform Hatfield who used these manuscripts in his 1941 edition, but who in 1923 had to be content with printed versions or Shorter's inferior transcriptions.

It may be asked why if Hatfield knew that Shorter was so incompetent he allowed Shorter with Hodder & Stoughton, as he later allowed Wise and Symington with the Shakespeare Head, to use his work for their own ends. The answer lies partly in Hatfield's own temperament: a shy, retiring man with an exacting career in the Civil Service he never sought the limelight, and was quite content that his private hobby should be rewarded by correct texts of the Brontës appearing. Professional scholars could, but rarely do, emulate such altruism. Hatfield could only get his work published under Shorter's name because of Shorter's claim to own the copyright of all unpublished Brontë manuscripts.

This claim was based on Shorter's view that he had bought the copyright from Mr Nicholls. Correspondence between Mr Nicholls and Shorter in the Brotherton Collection at Leeds shows that Mr Nicholls was either unwilling to sell, or unaware of what he had sold. Hatfield was frequently indignant about Shorter's alleged ownership of the copyright. On 12 August 1926 he said it was absurd that Shorter should have control of manuscripts of which he knew nothing, although grudgingly admitting that Shorter did have some kind of rights over the manuscripts, of which he had originally made transcripts. He said the same on 7 April 1926, although pointing out regretfully that Hodder & Stoughton were unlikely to bring out a book of Brontë poetry not by Shorter as Sir Ernest Hodder Williams was a friend of Shorter's. After Shorter's death neither his executors nor his widow were reluctant to give permission for unpublished Brontë manuscripts to be published, and we find Hatfield chivalrously worried about Romer Wilson who was anxious to include some new versions of Emily's poetry in her *All Alone*. Eventually on 13 March 1928 Hatfield obtained permission to print anything he liked from Mrs Shorter, although he only seemed to have exercised this right in publishing a new version of Emily's poems.

Hatfield's correspondence is not just a list of complaints. Indeed these are remarkably restrained. We also have some invaluable remarks on Brontë poetry and prose, both of a textual and of a critical nature. The latter are perhaps the most gratifying, as sometimes Hatfield has the reputation of not caring what the Brontës wrote provided that the text was correct. He has no time for those like Alice Law who maintained that Branwell could have written *Wuthering Heights*, pointing out very shrewdly some close parallels between the work and Emily's poetry. On the other hand, Branwell is seen as a better poet than either Charlotte or Anne in a letter of 9 January 1926, and on 3 February 1926 Hatfield says that had Branwell been properly tutored he would probably have proved the greatest genius in the family. Charlotte's poem 'We wove a web of childhood' is dismissed as of small literary worth but considerable biographical significance in a letter of 7 February 1928. Extravagant claims for Branwell's and Charlotte's juvenilia are met by Hatfield calling *The Green Dwarf* and *The Foundling* by Charlotte schoolgirl nonsense and dismissing some of Branwell's early writing as rubbish. On the other hand, Emily's skill as a poet is acknowledged, and again and again we see Hatfield rejoicing that the Honresfeld manuscript gave a better reading than earlier transcripts or printed texts, some of which had accepted bowdlérisations by Charlotte which do also appear in pencil on this manuscript.

As a textual editor Hatfield is not perfect. He adopts an eclectic attitude to the Brontës' eccentric punctuation. In the Henry Huntington Collection the manuscript of 'We wove a web of childhood' contains a transcript which appears to be in Hatfield's handwriting; neither the transcript nor the difficult printed text of this poem is accurate, each containing roughly six mistakes in 230 lines. Some of Hatfield's conjectures about authorship are mistaken: there is in the Berg Collection a manuscript entitled 'To the Horse I rode at the battle of Zamorna' which is clearly in Emily's handwriting, although Hatfield attributed it to Branwell on the grounds that Emily never wrote about Zamorna. Sometimes we feel Hatfield is almost falling into Shorter's mistake of thinking that his transcripts were in some sense superior to the manuscripts. The latter were difficult to read, and widely scattered, whereas as he says in a letter of 26 September 1926 his transcripts were of particular value in that they united what had been divided. Elsewhere Hatfield is more sensible, as when in a letter of 12 June 1926 he cleverly distinguishes between Emily's and Charlotte's handwriting with particular reference to the letters w, th, g, y and p, and when he says in a letter of 13 April 1926 that if there is more than one version of a Brontë poem it is his duty to print the latest.

Hatfield's incidental comments are illuminating. He notes on 29 May 1926 that Mr Nicholls cannot have left the Brontë manuscripts untouched, as he copied some of Emily's poems, and gave some manuscripts to his cousins. He says on 6 December 1926 that the Brontë Society was in this period going through a bad period, as the original officials had either died or left, and there seemed a lack of enthusiasm and unselfishness in the work of the Society. In the same letter Symington whose part in editing the Brontë manuscripts is almost as suspect as that of Wise and Shorter is said to be energetic but with small knowledge of the Brontë literature and story. Fannie Ratchford is referred to somewhat patronisingly as a most sensible and enthusiastic Brontë student (15 July 1926) who has done very well for a first attempt, although her typescript is full of errors (12 August 1926). The story of Bonnell's legacy to the Brontë Museum of his manuscripts and of Mrs Bonnell's reluctance to part with them is told slightly sardonically in a series of letters. Haworth was thought by Mrs

Bonnell and indeed by Hatfield to be an out of the way place, although on 27 February 1927 Hatfield does proudly point out that it had five thousand visitors a year.

This is a far cry from the world of 1982, and there are other remarks made by Hatfield which seem curiously anachronistic and which show that life was much more difficult in 1927 for the scholar than it is now. He notes that Miss Ratchford is speaking in Harvard and says that it is a long way from Texas to Harvard. So it is, but it is now possible to fly almost as quickly between these points as it is to go by train from Hatfield's home in Kidderminster to London. And it is possible, *crede experto*, to draw on research and university funds to make these long journeys, whereas Hatfield had no such resources on which to draw. Perhaps it was lack of money as much as of time that prevented Hatfield from going to London and copying the Brontë manuscripts in the British Museum. He admits he has not done this on 29 March 1926. Even more surprising is his confession that he had not noted that the edition of Emily's poems by Shorter in 1910 contained facsimiles of poems which he had copied down wrongly in 1923; this is because he did not possess, and could not get hold of a copy of the 1910 edition. Perhaps the most poignant remark of the whole correspondence comes when on 9 September 1926 he asks what a photostat is.

Later Hatfield for obvious reasons became very enthusiastic about photostats. One wonders what he could have done in an age where research grants, libraries, easy travel, sabbatical leave and the Xerox machine are taken for granted by most scholars. Those of us who have these advantages can but admire the unselfish devotion to his task which Hatfield has provided for Brontë students to emulate.

As it was, Hatfield had to hand over much of his work into less worthy hands. The full story of how Wise and Symington of all people were chosen to edit the Shakespeare Head edition has yet to be written, but there is some interesting correspondence between Wise and Symington in the Humanities Research Center at the University of Texas. Initially the edition appears to have been held up by someone called by Wise cautiously on 27 November 1931 as that 'd——d old woman'. Possibly this was a member of the Smith family refusing permission to reprint the Brontë novels; there are references by Wise on 12 January 1932 to Miss Ethel Murray Smith, and by Symington on 23 November 1931 to a terrible woman at Menston asylum. Initially, as Symington says on 23 March 1931, the edition was intended to occupy 11 volumes. Interestingly, both Symington and Wise dismiss Shorter's claims to copyright. Wise says on 6 April 1931 that Symington need have no fear regarding the Shorter copyright claims, which Symington on 23 March says is regarded by quite a number of people as 'bunkum'.

Symington's tone to Wise is sycophantic, whereas Wise is curt. With Carter and Pollard on his trail Wise took refuge in ill health, and there are some rather pathetic letters from Wise's nurse and wife regretting that Wise is too ill to conduct a proper correspondence. In spite of Symington's hypocritical references to Wise's wonderful advice and help (4 October 1931) as editor-in-chief, it is clear that Symington did most if not all of the work. Hatfield sent two polite letters to Wise, also preserved in Texas, saying on 17 May 1929 he had abandoned work on the Brontës, but on 22 May of the same year offering some advice on the authorship of 'The Wanderer'. In 1932 Symington writing to Wise mentions Hatfield three times. On 11 January Hatfield is said to be disgusted with the Brontë Society, on 8 July he is reported as refusing help with the Brontë poems, but on 22 November Symington declares that Hatfield writes charming letters.

The correspondence between Symington and Wise peters out disappointingly in 1933; we hear about the sale of the Honresfeld manuscripts on 20 March, and on 27 July Symington expresses the hope, never really fulfilled, that Branwell's poems will be something of a sensation. In 1934 the long-gathering storm prepared by Carter and Pollard finally broke, and the only note at Texas of relations between Symington and Wise is a rather macabre account of Wise's funeral in 1937, attended by remarkably few mourners. Symington was one of these mourners, and he does seem to have inherited Wise's mantle in more than one way. The magnificent Symington Collection at Rutgers University contains an invaluable assembly of letters to Wise about English literary figures: typically it is not quite as strong in Brontë items as was originally promised by Professor Leslie Marchand in an enthusiastic article in the *Rutgers University Journal*.[2] Symington had disposed of most of his Brontë collection elsewhere; one wonders what his claim was to the items he had acquired.

NOTES

1. In re-editing Branwell's poetry for Blackwell I have been greatly helped by a typescript of Hatfield's in the Brontë Parsonage Museum.
2. L. Marchand, 'The Symington Collection', *Rutgers University Journal* (1948) pp. 1–15.

3 Early Brontë Chronology

EDWARD CHITHAM

For almost as long as people have excitedly read *Jane Eyre* or *Wuthering Heights* they have been intrigued by the authors of those novels. Attempts were soon made to unravel the mystery of the three Bells (or were they all one?) and to understand the characters and motivation of writers who could produce such an unusual clutch of novels and poems. This public found its thirst quenched by the masterly Elizabeth Gaskell, yet a significant trickle of better-off enthusiasts continued to board trains for Keighley and hire conveyances up to Haworth to see if they could catch sight of old Mr Brontë being led across the churchyard to take a service in the building where his two most famous daughters were buried.

Old Mr Brontë died, but the stream of visitors continued, and Mrs Gaskell, like the Brontë sisters, continued to be read. There were no further major revelations until Clement Shorter went to Ireland to coax from Charlotte's husband the drawings and scraps of poems he had hidden away, with the Brontë juvenilia, ever since his wife had died. This material was destined for the fire, but Shorter saved it. Soon the reading public became aware of a hinterland of secret Brontë writings, which were slowly released in a continuous but sluggish stream of limited editions, while every now and then there was a sale of manuscripts, duly borne away by their new owners to find a long resting place in private library or bank vault. Meanwhile, Shorter added his own books to the monographs produced on Charlotte and Emily, and the biographical tone was set.

Scholars may find this biographical emphasis unpalatable, and there are times when one feels that searches for the original Thornfield, or Thrushcross Grange, are totally irrelevant. But in other areas, a background of the authors' lives may be of great help in understanding the works. In the case of Emily Brontë the relationship between her life and her poetry has been a constant source of dispute, and this is quite understandable. For if we cannot be sure whether to read a given verse as a personal statement or a Gondal fiction, we may completely miss the tone of the poem.

Hardly had the Brontë Society been set up in 1896 when it began issuing 'Brontë Chronologies', which with modifications have persisted to this day. The trouble with these chronologies is that they are based on very little firm evidence. At the root of most is the series of letters which Charlotte sent to her close friend Ellen Nussey. There may have been five hundred of these left after Charlotte's death, and Mrs Gaskell quoted from a substantial number in her *Life of Charlotte Brontë*, as has every subsequent biographer. Of these letters there is no satisfactory text. The preparation of such a text is a lifetime's work, and in the meantime the most accessible place where a considerable number of the letters is collected is the Shakespeare Head *The Brontës*, edited by T. J. Wise and J. A. Symington in the the 1930s.

Much of this work is a compilation, based on earlier editions of Shorter and Hatfield, with notes transferred *en bloc* and no clear indication of sources. Charlotte's letters to Ellen tend not to appear chronologically, but by subject: in this respect the edition followed the trend set by Shorter in his *Charlotte Brontë and her Circle* of 1896. Texts of the letters are haphazard and dates capricious. A peppering of square brackets and notes gives a plausible air of scholarship, yet when one looks in the manuscripts for some of the dates that are printed in the Shakespeare Head edition they are nowhere to be found.

In the ensuing article I propose to discuss the period 1836–40 in the light of the MSS letters and external evidence. The major gain will be a positive solution to the well-known 'Law Hill problem', enabling us to see for certain whether the dates of the poems alleged to be written at Law Hill are composition or transcription dates. The following questions will be considered, and the dates of each discussed, so that in some cases traditional chronology will be disturbed. In other cases we shall see that confidently asserted dates rest on no evidence, and that there is a need for further research to try to discover reliable grounds for reconstruction.

The matters and dates in question are as follows:

   (i) When did Emily go to Law Hill, Halifax, as a teacher? How long did she stay in this position? Were her poems dated December 1838 written at Law Hill or elsewhere?

  (ii) When did Tabitha Aykroyd, the Brontës' old servant, slip in the village street and damage her leg? Mrs Gaskell gives the date as December 1837, but this is modified in Shorter and the Shakespeare Head edition to 1836.

(iii) When did Charlotte leave Miss Wooler's school? Biographers
       often say June 1838, but as we shall see there is evidence that
       she was there in the autumn, and a letter of January 1839 has
       been widely misunderstood.

(iv)   Is there any evidence to support the traditional chronology of
       the first month or two in 1840; Branwell's post at Broughton,
       the lectures given by William Weightman, the dispute over
       church rates, etc.?

In addition, there are a number of traditional dates during the period
which cannot be clearly substantiated and which raise questions to
which answers are not yet forthcoming. All one can say is that there is
need for greater caution than biographers traditionally exercise in
quoting these dates. Among these are:

(v)   The date of Ellen Nussey's move from Rydings to Brookroyd.

(vi)   The date of Miss Wooler's move from Roe Head to Dewsbury
       Moor.

(vii) Anne's illness (illnesses?) while at Miss Wooler's school.

In her well-known introduction to 'Selections from Poems by Ellis
Bell', published in 1850, Charlotte Brontë makes statements which
pose a number of difficulties to Brontë biographers.

'I venture to give three little poems of my sister Emily's, written in
her sixteenth year,' writes Charlotte, 'because they illustrate a point in
her character.' Emily's sixteenth year was between July 1833 and July
1834. None of the poems given in Charlotte's text date from this year
or anywhere near it. Charlotte finishes her introduction with this
sentence: 'The following pieces were composed at twilight, in the
schoolroom, when the leisure of the evening play-hour brought back in
full the thoughts of home.' She then prints three poems from the MS
Hatfield classified as A: A2, A4 and A1, all dated in the handwriting of
Emily Brontë November or December 1838 (numbered in Hatfield's
1941 edition 92, 94 and 91 respectively. Hereafter I shall refer to
Emily's poems by Hatfield's numbers, prefixed with the letter H).

There can be no real doubt about these dates in the MS, though to
the hasty eye the final 8 in H92 might just be mistaken for a 3. It can be
admitted that a single careless glance at this date might lead to the
assumption that it was indeed written by Emily 'in her sixteenth year'.
It may also be significant that it is this poem which Charlotte prints
first, though it is not the first in MS order.

However, Emily Brontë was never at school during her sixteenth year, 1833–4. She appears to have been at Roe Head, Miss Wooler's school, as a pupil during part of the autumn of 1835, and authorities generally say that in October 1837 (Emily's nineteenth year) she took up a teaching post at Law Hill, near Halifax, which was run by a Miss Patchet or Patchett.

This period of Emily's life is very ill-documented, and, the moment one begins to probe, contradictions appear. Yet it would be valuable to know more about it, since it is often supposed that Emily stayed long enough at Law Hill to learn the story of a local character of the past, one Jack Sharp, whose intrigue is said to be one basis for *Wuthering Heights.* Hilda Marsden, following Charles Simpson and an early writer in *The Bookman*, persuasively identifies the geography of Southowram and Shibden with that of the novel.[1] Emily's first biographer, Miss A. M. F. Robinson, while neither confirming nor denying the date of Emily's departure for Law Hill, says that she persisted there during the autumn term and then returned to Haworth for Christmas. After that she 'again left it for the hated life she led, drudging among strangers'. In spring, however, 'her health broke down, shattered by long-resisted homesickness. Weary and mortified at heart, Emily again went back to seek life and happiness on the wild moors of Haworth.'[2] This account is attached to a chapter concerned with events culminating at midsummer 1836, so that although no date is given for Emily's stay at Law Hill the impression is given that it took place during the end of 1836 and beginning of 1837.

Miss Winifred Gerin, writing in 1971, argues that the period of six months' absence suggested by Miss Robinson is correct, but cites the opposition evidence from a Mrs Watkinson of Huddersfield, reported by Mrs Chadwick in *In the Footsteps of the Brontës*, the text of which is as follows:

> Mrs Watkinson of Huddersfield, who first went as a pupil to Law Hill in Oct., 1838, has kindly allowed me to see letters of hers written at that time from Law Hill, and she is absolutely certain that Emily Brontë was a teacher during the winter, 1838–39; she remembers her quite well and one thing that impressed her most about Emily Brontë was her devotion to the house-dog, which, she once told her little pupils, was dearer to her then they were.[3]

Miss Gerin considers that Emily arrived at Law Hill about the end of September or beginning of October 1837, and points to the picture of

Keeper, Emily's dog, done on 24 April 1838 'from life' as evidence that by this time Emily had left Law Hill and was back home.[4] This picture is also regarded as important by F. B. Pinion. We thus have a weak early tradition that Emily went to Law Hill in 1836 and a slightly stronger assertion that she stayed for six months, confronted by Mrs Watkinson's contrary evidence, apparently supported by letters (now untraceable) dating her encounter with Emily to 1838–9.

At this point we turn to Charlotte's claim in the 1850 introduction that these three poems, dating from 1838, were composed 'in the schoolroom', and the content of the poems which on the face of it supports Charlotte's claim. Even if Charlotte is wrong about the date ('her sixteenth year'), as I have shown she must be, she could be right about the place of composition. A way might be found out of the difficulty by supposing the 1838 date to be a transcription date. Miss Gerin toys with this idea, and points to the strength of the 'six months' tradition, citing Gaskell and Leyland as well as Miss Robinson.[5] Leyland's account is indeed worth noting, for although he unfortunately gives no date, his support of the 'six months' tradition is apparently based on another fresh source:

> Her extreme reserve with strangers is remembered by *one who knew her there*, but she was not at all of an unkindly nature; on the contrary, her disposition was generous and considerate to those with whom she was on familiar terms: her stay at Law Hill terminated *at the end of six months*.[6] [My italics]

It must be remembered that Leyland had strong Halifax connections, and this account sounds as if it is derived from an ex-pupil. The 'transcription date' theory is very weak, however, for there is no case of Emily attaching a transcription date to a poem instead of a composition date. In fact, where multiple copies of poems exist the dates tally, showing that the poem is transcribed without change of date. It must be recalled that Hatfield's A MS does carry a transcription date, clearly so designated at the head: 'Transcribed Feb[r]uary 1844'.[7] So unless these three poems form a unique trio they were written in November–December 1838.

Charlotte's editing of the 1850 selection was a very hasty affair; so much so that she included two copies of the same poem of Anne's under two different titles without apparently realising this.[8] She also had a tendency to depreciate her sisters' capabilities as governesses, perhaps in compensation for her own guilt at being unsuccessful at working for anyone but Miss Wooler. She mentions only two periods when Emily was at school: this occasion, which has somehow become muddled with the Roe Head experience, and the Brussels sojourn, which she vaguely ascribes to 'after her twentieth year'.

Let us now state the 'Law Hill problem' in its clearest terms, preparatory to solving it. We are sure that Emily Brontë was a teacher at Law Hill school, near Halifax. Leyland, apparently on the authority of an ex-pupil, states 'her stay at Law Hill terminated at the end of six months'. Mrs Gaskell and Miss Robinson imply that this employment began in late 1836. Modern authorities, the two most recent being Miss Gerin and John Hewish, say that the year was 1837, but tend to support the 'six months' hypothesis.[9] On the other hand, we have the report by Mrs Chadwick that a former pupil remembered Emily at Law Hill in October 1838, and we have three poems which Charlotte tells us were composed in the schoolroom, dated at the end of that year.

This is indeed a riddle, yet we need to solve it in order to be in a position to interpret the poems clearly and to be sure whether they have a direct and personal contemporary reference or not. The riddle can be solved, but in doing so we shall find a number of long-accepted dates dislocated, and a considerable proportion of the chronology from 1836 to 1839 upset; nor will it be possible to reconstruct all this in the current examination, since the dislocation will affect Charlotte, Branwell and Anne as well as Emily. However, the solution will reconcile Mrs Watkinson's statement with Leyland and Robinson, and almost with Mrs Gaskell.

When traced to its source the idea that Emily went to Law Hill in October 1837 rests on one piece of evidence only. This is a letter of Charlotte to Ellen Nussey, headed in *SHBL* 'Dewsbury Moor, October 2nd, 1837', which contains the following sentence: 'My sister Emily is gone into a situation as teacher in a large school of near forty pupils, near Halifax.'[10] Mrs Gaskell, however, dates this letter 1836, and sure enough when the manuscript at BPM is examined, it bears the date 1836 in Charlotte's handwriting.

There are two pieces of evidence which conflict with this date, and one is forced to suppose that Charlotte simply wrote the wrong date (examination of the letter rids us of any idea that the 6 may be faded or altered). To begin with, in her 1841 diary paper (lost but quoted by Shorter) Anne Brontë lists among the 'diversities' she did not expect or foresee 'in the July of 1837' the fact that 'Emily has been a teacher at Miss Patchett's school and left it'.[11] When this paper was discovered, doubt was thrown on Mrs Gaskell's dating of 1836 for the letter. By the time of *SHBL* the date had been silently amended to 1837: yet as already stated, great problems are caused by dating the letter 1837, and there is no MS warrant.

Let us now move to the next part of the argument. To show that Charlotte was guilty of a small error in writing 1836 does not offer any indication that the correct number should be 7: it could as well be 8. A re-examination of letters adjacent to the 'Law Hill' letter may provide help. The letter of 2 October is preceded by one dated 24 August, and according to Shorter the year is 1837.[12] However, in reality the MS gives no year, as Miss Christian's Census correctly records.[13] Again we appear to have a silent drift to 1837. There are several links in subject matter with the 'Law Hill' letter, and I shall highlight two matters mentioned.

   (i) 'Mary Taylor is better and . . . she and Martha are gone to take
       a tour in Wales.' This links with the following information in
       the 'Law Hill' letter of 2 October: 'The Taylors have got home
       after their Welsh tour. They spent three weeks at Aberystwyth
       on the coast.'
  (ii) 'Miss Eliza Wooler and Mrs Wooler are coming here next
       Christmas. Miss Wooler will then relinquish the school in
       favour of her sister Eliza.' No mention is made of Mr Wooler;
       this is important as we shall see.

These two letters, then, both headed 'Dewsbury Moor', cohere. There is nothing in either to suggest that they belong to 1837. At this stage of the discussion one may increasingly be drawn to 1838 as a date; but this raises another problem in Charlotte's biography which cannot be ignored. From the point of view of Emily's life, transferring the letters to 1838 makes sense (and indeed a subsequently discovered piece of evidence will compel this conclusion). The evidence given in Gerin, suggesting that Emily was not at Law Hill in mid-1838 is not conclusive; the drawing of Keeper dated 24 April 1838 would not show that she had returned from Law Hill, but would be consistent with the view that she had not yet gone there.[14]

If we transfer the letters to 1838 we find that they are preceded by a letter of which the date is fairly certainly 9 June 1838. Among other things this letter records is that 'Mary Taylor is far from well', and it describes her high colour and fever. This looks like the beginning of the illness which was cured by a holiday in Aberystwyth. We may go on to question whether Margaret Wooler did in fact hand over her school to

Eliza at Christmas 1837. Apparently not, since she was giving Charlotte a present in May 1838. Mr Wooler died on 20 April 1838; this surely explains why he does not feature in the letter of 24 August as coming to Dewsbury Moor with his wife and daughter.[15]

So far we have found nothing to deter us from redating the crucial 'Law Hill letter' to 1838 instead of 1837. But there is a serious clash when we come to examine Charlotte's whereabouts during 1838. Most authorities regard June 1838 as the date when she ceased to work at Miss Wooler's school. If that date is correct, how can she be writing from Dewsbury Moor in August and October 1838?

Once again it seems as though rash assumptions may have been made on the basis of a letter of Charlotte's to Ellen. The letter in question is *SHBL* 68, already mentioned as the source of information about Mary Taylor's illness. There is no problem over the heading, which seems certain to be 'Haworth June 9th 1838'. 'You will be surprised', says Charlotte, 'when you see the date of this letter.' (She means, 'You will be surprised when you see the address'.) 'I ought to be at Dewsbury Moor, you know, but I stayed as long as I was able, and at length I neither could nor dared stay any longer. My health and spirits had utterly failed me ...'.

This remark of Charlotte's is usually taken to mean that at this point she finally retired from Dewsbury Moor, and it is linked with the gift of the book from Miss Wooler mentioned above. But Charlotte does not actually state any such thing. A little below she says: 'So home I went; the change has at once roused and soothed me, and I am now, I trust, fairly in the way to be myself again.' It seems certain that, by then thoroughly herself, Charlotte went back to Dewsbury Moor for Miss Wooler's final term, leaving when she handed over to her sister Eliza. Support for this view may be found by reinterpreting the letter to Ellen of 20 January 1839 in which she refuses an invitation to visit Brookroyd. She writes: 'Do you see nothing absurd in the idea of a person coming again into a neighbourhood within a month after they have taken a solemn and formal leave of all their acquaintance?' Gerin supposes the remark to mean that Charlotte had been to visit Brookroyd 'during December'.[16] But it may be that the words 'a solemn and formal leave of all their acquaintance' would accord better with a description of Charlotte's final departure from Dewsbury Moor (less than four miles from Brookroyd) after three-and-a-half years' teaching for Miss Wooler.

The chronology for the years 1837–8, then, is capable of radical revision on the basis of redating and reinterpretation of Charlotte's letters. This reconstruction follows from the redating of Charlotte's letter of 2 October, which she herself dated 1836, not to 1837 as does *SHBL*, but to 1838.

Luckily this letter is quite easily available at BPM, and it is there possible to see plainly a small shred of evidence on the letter itself which had it been noted earlier would have stopped the Shakespeare Head editors in their tracks and solved the Law Hill problem years ago. Many of Charlotte's letters to Ellen were sent by hand and therefore have no postmark by which their date can be checked. But in October 1838 Ellen was in Bath, and the letter had to be sent through the Post Office. It bears a postmark, admittedly a little difficult to see, since the letter has been mounted on card. The postmark reads '[DEWS]BURY OC 6 1838'.

There should, then, be no further problem about the date at which Emily Brontë went to Law Hill. She will have gone there at the end of September 1838, taught Mrs Watkinson, as that lady said, during October of that year and returned after about six months, as Leyland says, about March 1839 just before Anne set out for Blake Hall. We may here turn to the account of Miss A. M. F. Robinson, remembering that she talked to Haworth residents, asking questions specifically about Emily as Mrs Gaskell did not. Miss Robinson writes:

> She stood it, however, all that term; came back to Haworth for a brief rest at Christmas, and again left it for the hated life she led, drudging among strangers. But when spring came back, with its feverish weakness, with its beauty and memories, to that stern place of exile, she failed. Her health broke down, shattered by long-resisted homesickness. Weary and mortified at heart, Emily went back to seek life and happiness on the wild moors of Haworth.[17]

The poems supposed to have been written 'in the schoolroom' will thus have been composed at Law Hill. The MS dates will be composition dates, not transcription dates; the poems reflect actual contemporary events in Emily's circumstances. It remains to be seen whether in the future some further evidence will be discovered to support the indications in such widely divergent writers as Hilda Marsden and Romer Wilson that these six months played a crucial part in the fruition of Emily's art, in respect of the novel as much as the poetry.

Once we have realised that the chronology given to Charlotte's letters in *SHBL* is highly suspect and that dates given at the headings, even sometimes without square brackets, may be pure conjecture, we may be inclined to treat the chronological 'facts' given by many biographers with great scepticism. As has been shown, the chronology of Law Hill is different from what has been stated in the accounts of most writers, and no biographer at all has so far noticed the real purport of Charlotte's letter of January 1839, which in conjunction with the redated Law Hill letter shows she stayed with Miss Wooler until December 1838.

We turn next to the disputed date of Tabitha Aykroyd's fall in the village street of Haworth and consequent rest from work at the parsonage. The letter containing this news is at BPM. In reviewing it in after years Ellen Nussey has written the date 'Dec 29 – 37' on it, and Mrs Gaskell has accepted that date as she accepted so many from Ellen. However, the letter is postmarked BRADFORD YORKS DE 29 183 only: the Post Office official, using the hand date stamp, has omitted to insert the final digit.

In her usual haphazard way Charlotte herself has not dated the letter at all. However, it is possible to decide which year the accident happened on internal evidence, and in fact one can discover almost certainly the date of the evening when the fall happened. First, however, we need to deal with a chronological red herring. In addition to the date stamp applied by the counter staff at Bradford, there is on this letter (as on many letters of Charlotte's about this time) a further rubber stamp reading 'Bradford Yor[ks] Penny Post'. It may be thought that this implied a date after, or at least near, 1840, when the Penny Post is known to have been introduced. However, the main points of the 1840 reform were *prepayment* for the fee, *standardisation* at one penny, and the introduction of a stamp to show that payment had been made. The *Bradford Observer* of 30 January 1840 describes alterations to the counter being made at the local Post Office in consequence of the new system. But there is evidence to show that Bradford, like a number of centres in various parts of the country, ran a penny post system for some years before 1840. There is no need therefore to suppose that this letter of Charlotte's must be dated on or after 29 December 1839.

Within the letter Charlotte mentions that 'the moors are blockaded with snow'. Abraham Shackleton, recording the weather in his observatory at Braithwaite, Keighley, three miles from Haworth, saw 'some snow' on 14 December 1837, but then the weather turned mild. On

20 December there was a great deal of rain, resulting in flooding, but no more snow. He summarises the month saying 'This month has been mild for the season'. Charlotte cannot have written the letter in December 1837, as Mrs Gaskell said, and as Ellen Nussey had inaccurately remembered.

But December 1836 was a very different month. The *Philosophical Magazine* for January–June 1837 comments:

> The heavy snow storm, which, at London, commenced on the 25th [December], is perhaps the most remarkable of any recorded at the same period of the season. It appears to have been general, not only over Britain, but also over a great part of Europe.

Records at Boston, Lincs., show snow beginning on the afternoon of 24 December and continuing during the next two days, so that at the end the snow was 'drifted in some places ten feet deep'. At Braithwaite Shackleton prosaically records 'much snow' on 24 December, with more snow and wind on the next three days. There was no snow in the Keighley area in the relevant periods of 1838 or 1839. It is the year 1836 which closely accords with Charlotte's description of the moors 'blockaded with snow'. In this instance, weather records vindicate the guess of the *SHBL* editors, not that of Ellen Nussey.

We may go further, and make an informed conjecture at the actual date when Tabby fell in the frosty street. It was, Charlotte says, 'a few days after my return home [from Roe Head]'. The impression gained in the letter is that between then and the date of Charlotte's writing a fair period of time had elapsed, during which Tabby had been looked after at the parsonage. Shackleton's records show that the only day on which the temperature had been below freezing was Thursday 15 December, when the thermometer registered 29° F. By the following day the frost had abated.

Charlotte apparently returned from Roe Head on Wednesday 14 December, the date of Anne's good conduct prize awarded by Miss Wooler, and the conjectural date of *SHBL* letter 54. Although this was not 'several days' before 15 December, there is certainly no other day when the weather was frosty enough to cause a fall, and one must therefore allow Charlotte the benefit of novelist's licence. Tabby had fallen in the icy street on the evening of 15 December, about one-and-a-half days after Charlotte's return.

The early part of 1840 is an interesting period in Brontë history, when Anne moved towards personal poetry, Branwell left for his tutorship in Cumbria, Ellen Nussey visited Haworth and received a valentine from William Weightman (as did the other girls) and Emily wrote a mysterious personal poem, erroneously thought by some to have a Gondal reference, in which she beseeches a 'shade' to visit her during the dark hours before the dawn. Some of the traditional chronology is clearly wrong, and one looks for external evidence to confirm the witness of Charlotte's letters.[18]

For example, it is quite impossible to accept the Shakespeare Head edition dating for letter 86, in which Charlotte confirms Ellen's visit for 'Friday week'. If this had really been written on 29 December 1839, the letter dated 12 January 1840 could not be correct, but here the Shakespeare Head is on firmer ground, describing the Bradford postmark accurately. It is clear from letter 91 that Ellen was at Haworth on St Valentine's Day, 14 February. The Shakespeare Head dating of letter 86, in which Branwell is said to be setting out within the next few days for his post as private tutor in Ulverston must have been influenced by an incorrect inference from Branwell's own letter (*SHBL*, 90) in which he describes his night's fun on the way there. Though the activities of the evening look like New Year's Eve, they cannot be. All the evidence within the Brontë history alone points to the conclusion that 1 January would be a most unusual day for a tutor or governess to take up a post: as with school terms, tutorial contracts seem to date from about 20 January (see, for example, notices of reopening of 'academies' on the front page of the *Halifax Guardian*).

On the other hand the content and therefore dating of letter 92 is strongly confirmed by the *Bradford Observer* of 2 April 1840. Charlotte's 'stormy meeting' in which Mr Collins, Mr Weightman and Mr Brontë faced a crowd of dissenters to defend Church rates is reported in detail. It took place in the National School, and the debate lasted 'for three hours'. However, Charlotte interestingly does not mention the outcome, giving the impression that the church clergy carried the day. The *Observer* records:

A motion was passed by a very great majority that no church rate be granted for the chapelry. To extricate the churchwardens, who have bills against them to the amount of £21, it was agreed that collections be made in the church, and that dissenters help to pay off the debt.

This sounds like a decent British compromise, but one would not obtain a balanced view from Charlotte's letter. We need to remember Charlotte's partial views and her novelist's eye when we use her letters alone (as we are so often forced to do) as the basis of our evidence for events in the Brontë household. In this instance external material supports the dating of the letter, but not its purport; whereas we must reluctantly reject the traditional date of Branwell's departure for Cumbria.

Three other matters find as yet no certain chronological place. Letter 47, written in late May 1836 (Whit-Sunday was 22 May), proposes a stay 'at Rydings'. Letter 46, however, at the Henry Huntington Library, is addressed to Ellen at Brookroyd. The 'stormy evening' mentioned in the first paragraph suggests that it may have been written in autumn or later. In any case, it cannot be dated earlier than no. 47. One would like to know from external evidence when Ellen moved from Rydings to Brookroyd; so far no such evidence is forthcoming.

Another important event in Charlotte's life was the move from Roe Head to Dewsbury Moor, the date of which is shrouded in mystery. Biographers vaguely date this 1837, but this may be on the evidence of the letter of 2 October, which I have now shown dates from 1838. Charlotte's 'Confession of my Xtian faith' is dated at Roe Head, 29 May 1837, while letter 63, at Henry Huntington, has no address at the heading, though it was evidently written at school, not Haworth ('with Miss Wooler's leave'). It is unlikely that the school had moved within these ten days, and the event is not mentioned in the letter. No. 62, allegedly enclosed in no. 63, is labelled 'Roe Head' in Shorter's *Lives and Letters*, and the 'Dewsbury Moor' probably has no foundation; the MS is not traceable at the moment. It is possible, then, that Miss Wooler moved her school in summer 1837, but there is no positive evidence of Dewsbury Moor until 1838. It is by no means certain, despite the biographers' assertions, that Anne Brontë ever saw Dewsbury Moor, and her illness at Miss Wooler's school in late autumn 1837 may be the same that James de la Trobe mentioned in his letter to William Scruton (*BST*, vol. VIII), specifically mentioning Roe Head.

I hope that by now I have written enough to show that many chronological details in the years 1836–40 need challenging, and that some new answers can be found. There is however great need for other external sources, probably very trivial, to come to light before we can fix for certain dates in the Brontë calendar which may have had considerable effect on the writers' work.

NOTES

1. H. Marsden, 'The Scenic Background of *Wuthering Heights*', *BST*, vol. LXVII (1957) pp. 111–30.
2. A. Robinson, *Emily Brontë* (London, 1883) pp. 60, 82–4.
3. E. Chadwick, *In the Footsteps of the Brontës* (London, 1914) pp. 123–4.
4. W. Gerin, *Emily Brontë* (Oxford, 1971) p. 70.
5. Ibid., p. 83.
6. F. Leyland, *The Brontë Family* (London, 1886) p. 153.
7. Classification of MSS is taken throughout the sections of this book dealing with Emily Brontë from C. W. Hatfield, *The Complete Poems of Emily Jane Brontë* (Oxford, 1941).
8. E. Chitham, *The Poems of Anne Brontë* (London, 1979), pp. 94–5.
9. J. Hewish, *Emily Brontë* (London, 1969) p. 46.
10. *SHBL*, vol. I, p. 162.
11. C. K. Shorter, *Charlotte Brontë and her Circle* (London, 1896) p. 149.
12. Ibid., p. 177.
13. M. Christian, 'Census of Brontë Manuscripts', *The Trollopian*, vol. III (1949) pp. 55–72.
14. W. Gerin, *Emily Brontë*, p. 84.
15. His death is recorded in the *Halifax Guardian* for 1 May 1838 as having taken place on 20 April 1838.
16. W. Gerin, *Charlotte Brontë* (Oxford, 1967) p. 123.
17. Robinson, *Emily Brontë*, p. 60.
18. The poem is no. 134 in Hatfield's edition. Hereafter, poems will be referred to by their number prefixed with the letter H. Further reference will be made to the present poem in Chapter 6.

4 The Inspiration for Emily's Poetry

EDWARD CHITHAM

A little of the writing habits of the two younger Brontë sisters at an early period can be learned from the 1837 diary paper, though unfortunately it illuminates Anne more than Emily.[1] The paper is headed 'Monday evening June 26 1837', and it becomes clear later that 'evening' means about 4 o'clock. The text is written round the edge of a rough sketch of the sisters at work. We therefore have both a verbal and visual picture of the scene. However, the paper needs to be used with caution as a basis for generalisation about Emily; it may reflect only the setting for her more public writing, shared openly with Anne.

The drawing shows a table, round which Anne and Emily sit, occupied with 'The Papers' which are in front of them. The sheets of paper shown are double folded sheets of normal size, not small scraps such as usually contain Emily's first poetic essays. They do however appear to be individual sheets or at least thin groups of sheets, not full booklets. Their repository is evidently 'The Tin Box', so labelled and resting on the table in front of Emily. This box appears larger than the small tin discovered by Mr Nicholls in which the diary papers themselves came to light. It seems likely to have been large enough to take comfortably the folded octavo pages on which the girls were writing. Emily draws herself from the back, as she does in other diary papers.

Turning to the text, we find that while Anne is writing a poem, identifiable among her known output, Emily is engaged on 'Agustus-Almedas life' [*sic*]. She gives details of the movements of a number of Gondal personalities. The paper finishes with a piece of dialogue, unfortunately rather ambiguous:

Anne well do you intend to write in the evening
Emily well what think you
     (we agreed to go out 1st to make sure if we Get into a humour
     we may stay in

The final word is almost illegible and the lack of punctuation makes interpretation hazardous, but we can perhaps deduce that writing, certainly of prose and probably of poetry, needed 'the humour' before it could begin.

This diary paper constitutes the chief piece of external evidence of Emily's writing habits. Happily, it can be supplemented by a careful examination of the draft manuscripts, and these may also throw light on her underlying assumptions about poetic composition. Her habit of destroying drafts when she had recopied and polished the poem detracts from such evidence, but we must be thankful that she was reluctant to destroy all unsuccessful or incomplete poems, evidently wishing to hoard even such fragments as contributing to her own record of her personality, though not for the public eye.

Two dated fragments and one undated may be of use in discovering clues concerning her thought and methods, after which it may be possible to apply these preliminary insights to other poems. The fragments chosen, using Hatfield's names for the manuscripts, are D14, a ragged and untidy piece of work written in ink and dated 'August 12th 1839'; E9, a pencil scrawl erroneously suspected by T. J. Wise of being one of Anne's poems, and dated 'Feb 27 1841'; and E19, a small pencil fragment without date.

The last mentioned begins, 'I've dried my tears and then did smile', giving a first person experience directly to the reader. This is immediately rejected in favour of 'She dried her tears and they did smile', in which the emotional tone is similar, but made more remote by the substitution of a third person for a first person narrator and producing a clash of feeling more radical than the first version, since it is now the onlookers, 'they', who are smiling, apparently in incomprehension. Line three of the poem ran originally 'How little dreaming all the while', but this is immediately crossed out in favour of 'A fond delusion all the while', which again strengthens the sense of incomprehension on the part of the onlookers.

We observe that Emily Brontë has altered her poem as a result of second thoughts in two ways: she has removed herself some way from the centre, since though authorial sympathy with the weeping girl is still strong, it is now distanced; and she has thrown the onus of misunderstanding on to the onlookers, not the subject. Her initial 'and then did smile' implies a deceptive cover by the weeping girl, similar to the mask which is worn by Anne Brontë's first person heroine in her poem, 'Maiden, thou wert thoughtless once' and at times in *Agnes Grey*.[2] In the second version, Emily Brontë upbraids the onlookers with their 'fond delusion'. Our initial fellow-feeling for the girl of the poem has been supplemented by alienation from the bystanders. It may indeed be that this phrase 'fond delusion' was felt by Emily to be too rhetorical, and this may have been one reason for the abandonment of the poem. This is not the only place where we may feel that she is trying to increase the loneliness and alienation of her hero or heroine in a way that rings false, by overstatement.

A rather similar movement from personal to impersonal is apparent in the poem on MS E9. Here we have a chained bird, often taken to be a hawk, standing almost as a symbol for the poet's consciousness. As the bird yearns for freedom so does the poet. This equation is unambiguously stated in line 1, 'And like myself lone wholly lone', and the first stanza is unaltered.

By the second four-line stanza Emily Brontë is becoming unsure of her pronouns. She has indeed established that the poet and the bird are at one, but again she wishes to conceal or play down the poet's own involvement. In stanza 2, line 3, 'I ask for nothing further here' perhaps becomes '*We* ask for nothing ...' and a parallel change is made in line 4, where 'my own heart' becomes 'our own heart'.

Stanza 3 began as a colloquy between the bird and the poet:

Ah could my hand unlock thy chain
How gladly would I see thee soar ...

which becomes

Ah could my hand unlock *its* chain
How gladly would I see *it* soar ...

This rejection of the second person, like the rejection of the first person in the other fragment studied, again involves Emily in retreat from immediacy. It removes the reader very slightly from the sharpness of the scene, and cools the poem. This particular work remains interesting, and we must clearly abide by Emily's second thoughts, even though she did not recopy the poem. Nevertheless, as in 'She dried her tears', we experience a slight withdrawal of the poet in studying the two versions. Similar withdrawals are to be met in a number of places where Emily revises and substitutes her second thoughts. It may well appear that in these two poems she first puts down on paper in rough an emotion she wishes to fix, then begins to adapt or alter it rationally, and in doing so retreats a little from her subject.

Turning now to the poem on MS D14, we find a paper beginning neatly, but soon faltering and then drawn over with many doodles of abstract or possibly symbolic designs. Though there are no speech marks, the poem seems to begin with a conversation. The tone of the first question sounds like real speech, 'How long will you remain?' The questioner points out that it is past midnight, the clock of the 'minster' having struck. Remembering that the hours of darkness at Haworth would be punctuated by the sound of the church clock – not indeed the present church clock, but an earlier one, the remains of which lingered around the premises until the 1930s – we have no difficulty in tracing the thoughts and feelings present at the start of the poem: Emily is sitting up at night and is being asked by a sister a straightforward question.[3] St Michael's Church becomes 'the minster' partly for reasons of romance, but we may also sense a little of the same withdrawal from the actual which we have seen in the other poems.

The speaker next urges the dying fire, the flickering lamp, heavy eyelids and cold hands as reasons for retiring, but the other person (surely Emily?) bursts out almost crossly, 'No leave me let me linger yet tis long', the forceful ls tumbling over themselves to be expressed. Emily's revision of the line smooths it somewhat to 'No let me linger leave me let me be', though it is not clear whether on this occasion any similar retreat to those previously mentioned is achieved. However, the mere fact that Emily thought the line ought to be revised is worth noting.

Of course, one cannot prove that this poem was actually written in the drawing room at Haworth just after midnight with the fire burning low in the grate: yet it seems rather perverse to deny such a likely inference. Such little external evidence as we have does suggest that the sisters would often stay up after Mr Brontë had retired to bed, and the large number of Emily Brontë's poems which have their setting at night gives the impression that she stayed awake a good deal.[4]

But as the poem proceeds it undergoes a transformation which I would suggest is very frequent in Emily's work, and which is an extension of the process we saw operating in the two previous small poems. At about line 19 the external landscape begins to be described,

'Look on those woods ...', but there are no woods at Haworth. If we have been reading the poem as a simple first-hand account of a late evening at Haworth parsonage the woods strike us with a note of incongruity. A few lines later there is a worse shock: a river is introduced. The poet's eye now perhaps glimpses a Gondal scene which is however not very clearly particularised, and ends on a Wordsworthian note as a lament for lost infancy.

The paper on which the poem is written gives evidence of a dreamy part-absorption in the work. The odd word 'Re-give', for example, used in the last line but one, is repeatedly scribbled on the paper below the poem, as though Emily becomes hypnotised by her own invention. The doodles on the right-hand side and under the poem have no coherence or structure, consisting in part of wavy lines and circles, and there is in addition an apparent name, perhaps 'Brymn', written in Emily's conventional handwriting, not small script. All in all, the paper does not give the appearance of close rational attention, but more of dreamy drift.

On the left-hand side of the paper are two slightly more coherent pictures, one apparently of a bunchy feather or possibly a cluster of pine needles, the other of a snake with dragon-like wings. One might perhaps recall the kind of dreamy sketch found in Shelley's notebooks.

A further example of the withdrawal process mentioned above may be provided by the change in line 9. It appears here that the second of two words crossed through originally read 'ghost'. For this word Emily substitutes the phrase 'happy dream', considerably weaker and more innocuous. If this nearly illegible word is 'ghost' then the drawing of a winged snake may represent it. This would not be Emily Brontë's only drawing of a ghost in her poetry MSS, since there is also the weird skull-like scrawl at the foot of MS E5, accompanying the lines:

> What Shadow is it
> That ever moves before my eyes
> It has a brow of ghostly whiteness.

Having mentioned the tiny fragment MS E5, it may be as well to remark the three poetic beginnings written on it. They are so tentative that they do not seem to have merited further work on them by the poet, who perhaps only kept the scrap of paper for the mysterious list of dates on it. But just because they are small fragments left incomplete when the inspiration ran out, they may be of help in building up a picture of Emily's methods.

The first beginning, dated 'November 23rd 1839', starts from an observation in itself entirely trivial:

> The wind was cruel which tore
> That leaf from its parent tree

The word 'cruel' is subsequently changed to 'rough', more expressive of the wind, so that in line 3 'cruel' can be applied to 'fate' without repetition. From the observation of the single leaf torn off by the wind Emily moves on to a reflection:

> The fate was cruel which bore
> Its withering corpse to me.

The lines impute an altogether unwarranted fierceness to the 'fate' in question, and illustrate a frequent characteristic of Emily Brontë's work, her exaggerated intensity of feeling over trivia.

The second and third beginnings on the paper are so slight as to be hard to interpret:

> We wander on we have no rest
> It is a dreary way.

This may be Emily's recollection of an afternoon on the moors or may be metaphorically describing her life. 'What Shadow is it?' quoted above, exhibits a rather surprising capital S, and asserts some kind of vision seen continuously by Emily; though of course the word 'ever' may be as hyperbolic here as the 'cruel' fate which blew one withered autumn leaf towards the poet in the previous fragment.

These beginnings of poems are then abandoned, and we may regard them as seeds of poems which did not germinate. Many another Emily Brontë poem begins with such a 'seed', consisting of a small sense impression followed by or accompanied by a mental reflection. Often the seed is characterised by a date which turns out to be the actual date of composition (e.g. B22 which later became 'A Farewell to Alexandria' begins, on 12 July 1839, 'I've seen this dell in July's shine'; C14, which later becomes 'Lines by Claudia' begins on 28 May 1839 – a 'very warm' day according to local weather records, 'I did not sleep; 'twas noon of day/I saw the burning sunshine fall').

It may appear that Emily Brontë often began her poems without the slightest idea how they would proceed, but with a sense impression or a record of a fact. Quite possibly these beginnings, which often give a feeling of good organisation and convey genuine depth of feeling, simply floated into her head and insisted on being written down. Then, after a few lines or in some cases a few stanzas, the inspiration died, and Emily was left with the problem of completing consciously what her subconscious mind had begun.

It was at this point or later that Gondal came into the matter.[5] These poetic seeds are not Gondal seeds. Gondal seems to be part of Emily's conscious mind in a way in which the 'ghosts' we have seen in the two fragments are not. There is a very frequent tendency in Emily's poems to move away from the real scene, her positive concern at the time, to a fake world of Gondal feeling or action. A clear example is the poem on B10, dated 17 April 1839, which gives the game away by its reference in stanza 2:

> Yet the grass before the door
> Grows as green in April rain . . .

The poem is a lament for cheer that has gone from 'our evening fireside', and is surely associated with the departure of Anne for Blake Hall. The first two verses are totally genuine, written in longing for her sister and regret at her absence; towards the end of the pair the poem moves to a vein of nostalgia for former April birdsong. In stanza 3 the poet ponders the reason for the eclipse of happiness, and in both this and stanza 4 we have a series of rhetorical questions which seem slack and vague, but do convey some sort of foreboding which might be associated with the departure of Anne for her first governess post, a kind of symbolic coming-of-age of the family. Stanza 5 begins:

> One is absent, and for one
> Cheerless, still is our hearthstone.
> One is absent . . .

But Emily's power and willingness to explore the emotional tones of this parting have now become exhausted. She moves hastily to Gondal, and the rest of the poem is little better than doggerel, exhibiting no particular poetic skill and not much feeling until the final stanzas.

Here then is an example of a poem beginning with a genuine subconscious poetic *donné*, then groping for continuation, finding a convenient but unexalted answer in Gondal, and so finished but not inspired. We find poem after poem among Emily Brontë's poetic output in which many stanzas are prosaic and pedestrian. Very often these prosaic stanzas are tricked out with Gondal names and narrative, showing that Emily used Gondal, a game originating in childhood, to avoid leaving pieces that were unfinished. She could indeed enjoy Gondal, but at a different level from her best poetry. Gondal had nothing intrinsically to offer to Emily Brontë as an auxiliary to her poetry, and in fact seems to provide only a retreat from confronting life and in many cases real feeling.

In addition to the revealing small fragments and beginnings of poems mentioned above there are a number of more lengthy drafts of poems, closely reworked, which may give some idea of how Emily Brontë approached poetic composition. It is only right to point out at the start, however, that these pieces are chiefly Gondal poems and there is no case of a draft remaining from a poem later finished and adjudged by critics to be among Emily's best work. Of the poems selected by Derek Stanford for inclusion in his category of 'major poems' only 'There let thy bleeding branch atone' exists in a rough and unpolished state, though there are late alterations to 'The Philosopher' and 'No coward soul is mine' which may be significant.[6] But we cannot discuss the technique adopted in the long drafts and significant re-workings we have without entering a caveat, that it is possible they represent an uninspired and workaday method of composition which may not have been characteristic of Emily at her best.

Nevertheless, the chronological span of these poems is considerable, and it may be that from them something can be deduced about Emily's attitude to the mechanics of poetic composition, though doubtless there would have been occasions when her subconscious processes could subsume and elevate this technical infrastructure. Such extensively reworked manuscripts still extant are D3 (1839), D15 (1840), E20 (1844), B44 (1846) and B45 (1848). A description of the revision techniques used here may help to show the poet's general method. The poems will be treated chronologically.

'Come hither child' (D3) is a powerful poem, though very flawed and technically imperfect. The subject of the poem is clear: a child has been able to play affecting music, which touched the heart of a lady in such a way that the lady enquires about the origin of this gift. The child answers by citing an occasion 'years ago' (altered to 'long ago') when she first heard angelic music on a 'windy night' and gained the gift of recalling and playing it. It does not appear that the poet's alterations make any major change in the story: on this occasion at any rate she knew what she was going to write about before she started.

The alterations in the first two stanzas substitute approximate equivalents. 'Waken' becomes 'rouse up', while 'years' becomes 'long'. The purpose of the alterations may have been to produce more telling sound:

> How daredst th*ou rou*se up thoughts in me

and

> Nay chide not *l*ady *l*ong ago.

In stanza 3 'But thus it was one windy night' becomes 'But thus it was one festal night', postponing the information that the wind was blowing and emphasising the party atmosphere. An alteration in stanza 5 substitutes a strong word for a weak, 'splendour' for 'pleas[ure]', but both enhance the feeling of outcast loneliness felt by the child. The stanza 6 alterations suggest first absent-mindedness ('god' is changed to 'God'), then a frequent indecision about demonstratives ('the' is changed to 'that'). The next stanza is harder to understand, since the erasures cannot all be restored; however it appears that Emily changed her mind in the direction of giving a little more detail about the actual experience, instead of moving towards the child's retrospective feeling. She discarded the first two lines of the verse when half written and began again.

The final stanza provides an alteration from 'spoke' to 'rose', which avoids alliteration with 'seraph strain', then a considerable reconstruction of the second line in which the noise 'died' instead of 'sank' and finally a rejection of the abstract 'thought' in the final line in favour of the warmer 'heart'.

It is not always possible to see that the poet's alterations have benefited this minor poem, and impossible to generalise on the nature of the changes made. There is a strong impression of attention being given to the work, and one concludes that the poet considered it worth the labour.

A second Gondal narrative is involved in 'Companions all day long we've stood' (D15). This exhibits seventeen changes to single words, some alterations of phrases, and three involving whole lines. In a thirteen-stanza poem the percentage of alterations involved is therefore quite high. In stanza 5 it seems that perhaps alterations were made to ensure a vague circular 'dreaminess' for a stanza about dreams. 'And all have seen of dreams' becomes first 'The bright fire brightly gleams' then 'The red fire brightly gleams', the 'red' of which is echoed in the next line.

In stanza 6 'I cannot trace' becomes 'I may not trace' and thus more remote, while in line 3 'as I can trace the storms fall' would not quite scan and is replaced by a line incorporating the poet's favourite 'ocean': 'As I can hear the oceans fall'. The point of the change in the next stanza is unclear: the couplet 'That makes his bounding pulse rejoice / And not *his* pulse alone' becomes 'That makes his bounding pulse rejoice / Yet makes not *his* alone' with a possibly unnecessary repetition.

In stanza 7, 'that' is changed twice to 'her', while an 'Eden' sky replaces a 'tranquil' sky. The choice of this adjective, with its overtones of a prelapsarian existence, may indicate the poet's feeling that Gondal is connected with childhood innocence, for all its wayward inhabitants.

The next two stanzas refine the account of the feelings of two children, Mary and Flora: second thoughts bring a gaze that is 'clouded pensively' and another 'may' for 'can'. As in the previous poem the alterations do not on the whole produce more vivid or detailed pictures and they sometimes seem like over-anxious tinkering with the lines.

'At Castle Wood' is another Gondal poem, appearing on MS E20. The first line exhibits a characteristic already seen in the smaller fragments; Emily Brontë begins:

> My task is done – the winter sun
> Is setting in its sullen sky

on a day when Shackleton's weather records say the weather was 'overcast' and there had been a 'good deal of snow at M[orning]'. It seems that on this Friday in early February Emily Brontë started by writing of herself as she looked out across the wintry landscape in late afternoon after finishing the day's work. But as in 'How long will you remain?' this first thought merges quickly with a Gondal scene.

The poem becomes one in which a Gondal character dreams gloomily of death. The letter formation in the manuscript is heavy and sloppy, suggesting that Emily shared fully in the gloom her pen expressed: as so often the Gondal character is merely a *persona*, voicing for a moment Emily's temporary feeling. 'My task is done' becomes the less personal 'The day is done'. Her biggest problem appears to have been to find lines suggesting the contrast between a happy and a gloomy spirit (stanza 5). The happy spirit is first characterised as 'dying hearts with pleasure glad' then something like 'hearts to happiness akin' and finally 'spirits born [of?] happiness', which may still not convey her meaning clearly since Hatfield reads 'born *for* happiness', though the letters do not seem to support the reading. This poem, however, is badly written and set out. A factor influencing her feeling at the time may possibly have been a reading of Keats: in this poem the misspelling 'brede' for 'bred', together with the expression 'foster child of sore distress' may suggest the presence in her subconscious mind of 'Ode on a Grecian Urn'.

The impression given by the altered beginning, the dull writing, the grammatical errors ('Through Life hard Task') and the struggle to express this contrast between spiritual life and death (as well as physical life and death) is that the poem's alterations are the result of a gradually formed conception, not a poem thought out previously, nor springing fresh and clear to the poet's mind, but one which struggled to birth on the paper itself.

Before looking at a final example of Emily at work on a poem, let us take the opportunity to enlarge a point made in reference to the last poem mentioned, 'At Castle Wood'. In this poem, as in 'How long will you remain?' Emily seems to have started with a phrase from life, accurately reflecting the actual present circumstances. This she does very often, using as a starting point a small observation of the external world (perhaps this is what is meant in the diary paper by 'getting into a humour'). Frequently the starting point is a weather observation, and it is this in part which has helped underpin Emily's reputation as a 'nature' poet. This reputation, though in part derived from metaphysical aspects of her poetry, is based on her ability to transmit the feel of Nature as exhibited by seasonal and especially climatic changes. It is a particularly English characteristic to be sensitive to weather and to the round of the seasons; with Emily Brontë these interests were a passion, not unconnected with her enthusiasm for dates themselves, which she shares with the other Brontës, especially Anne.

It is interesting to compare Emily Brontë as a nature poet with John Clare.[7] Throughout his poetry we note minute attention to weather, but we also find the names of species figuring throughout his work. Birds, flowers, trees are minutely observed with an accuracy that goes far beyond Emily Brontë. Even Anne Brontë introduces flower names into her work (verbena, daisy, buttercup, golden star, wallflower), but there is little such specific reference in Emily. Elm and pine are mentioned, with heath and harebell ('bluebell'), and birds are limited to a few, such as robin ('redbreast') and linnet (which linnet? Does she mean 'greenfinch' 'goldfinch' or 'common linnet'?). These references are increased if one takes *Wuthering Heights* into account, but in general we can say that at least in poetry Emily does not choose to be specific about the species of wildlife, though of course as a reader and copier of Bewick she must have known these species well. Instead we have lines like 'The mute bird sitting on the stone' and 'There are two trees in a lonely field'. It is not for her detailed observation of species that Emily Brontë may be called a nature poet. Birds, trees and flowers are used for the general atmosphere which they enhance: they are part of the landscape.

When we turn to the weather and the seasons, including the names of the months, the matter is different. Even a casual reader must be struck by the number of times the names of the months are found in Emily's verse. Wind, rain, sunshine, ice, snow; the poems are full of them, as is *Wuthering Heights*. Winter, summer, autumn (less often spring) occur in the following phrases: 'the summer day declines', 'the summer's day was done', 'golden summer's forests', 'autumn rain', 'summer morning', 'winter night', 'autumnal sky', 'summer evening' and many more. Most of the names of months occur, though October, November and December are the commonest.

It was Herbert Dingle who first suggested that a careful examination of these references to weather and internal date would yield information about the composition and intention of the poems. He goes so far as to suggest that Gondal poems may be sorted from non-Gondal by this method, and that Gondal poems will be found to be less dependent on current weather than non-Gondal poems. This suggestion does not seem to me to hold entirely; what is certain is that very frequently when we can check on the weather obtaining at the time of a poem being written by Emily on a known date, her poem will turn out to reflect the actual weather.

In order to substantiate this claim it will be necessary to discuss a number of references to weather in dated poems where we can be reasonably sure of the real weather at the time. This may appear a laborious proceeding, but in view of the scanty nature of external evidence relating to Emily Brontë's work the chance has to be grasped if we are to begin to understand the way in which her art begins from externals and moves inward.

Emily's poems reflect actuality in some of the following ways:

(i) Reference to a season which is the actual season of the poem;
(ii) Reference to a named month which is the actual month when the poem is written;

(iii) Reference to the moon as shining at night when we can show by reference to tables that it really shone on that night;

(iv) Reference to attested weather conditions such as rain, wind, bright or warm sunshine, snow, ice.

For external sources concerned with weather at the time we may go principally to the records of Abraham Shackleton of Braithwaite near Keighley, now at Cliffe Castle Museum and summarised by Herbert Dingle, supplemented by newspaper records and the Greenwich Observatory records published in the *Philosophical Transactions of the Royal Society*. These latter are fuller than the local records, but of course the discrepancy between Yorkshire weather and Greenwich weather can be considerable. Nevertheless, there is a considerable degree of correlation between Shackleton and Greenwich.

To begin with poems mentioning a specific season: summer is mentioned in poems 14 (July 1837), 18 (August 1837), 60 (May 1838), 65 (June 1838), 100 (May 1839), 103 (June 1839, 'this summer evening'), 113 (July 1839), 116 (August 1839), 139 (May 1840), 140 (September 1840), 147 (May 1841), 154 (August 1842), and also in 86 (November 1838, to lament the passing of summer), 94 (again lamenting that now 'The trees are bare, the sun is cold') and incongruously in 181 (February 1845).[8] Thus twelve poems where there is clear reference to summer weather were written between May and September, while only one was written out of season except the two which lament the absence of summer. Similarly autumn features in 31, 80, 91 and 120, all written in October or November, and winter in 93, 95, 127, 167, 177 and 179, all written between November and February.

More interesting still perhaps are the dated poems where the names of months occur. True, 7 (whose manuscript is not available for checking) refers to November but is apparently dated February, and 42, dated December, refers to September; but 61, dated 20 May 1838, refers to May; 63, dated 21 May 1838, talks of garlands woven for May by March; 97, dated 17 April 1839, talks of April rain; 101, dated 25 May 1839, begins 'May flowers are opening'; 108, dated 12 July 1839, begins, 'I've seen this dell in July's shine'; 175 and 177 are written in and mention October and November 1844 respectively, while 189 and 192 are written in and mention August (1845) and September (1846). Though 158 appears to be an exception, references to July and September lead to a reference to May, the date of writing. Poems 170 and 188, however, show that this generalisation cannot be made a universal rule.

It would unfortunately be impossible within the scope of this book to take each weather reference individually and show its relation to the ambient weather at the time. Dingle has published his findings, which need a little modification where Gondal poems are concerned.[9] From these it can be seen that such well-known poems as 'How clear she shines!' (157), and 'In summer's mellow midnight,/A cloudless moon shone through' (140) were actually written when the moon was almost full, and that even less known Gondal poems such as 179 ('The moon is full this winter night') have their origin in actuality. We can say that Emily Brontë is highly sensitive to weather conditions, frequently describes them accurately, and that in general the legends of the poetess gazing dreamily out of her bedroom window at the rain, wind or stars receive support when the poems and ambient weather are collated.

It would be a pity to conclude this essay on Emily Brontë's working methods without a glance at the last poem she wrote, the long Gondal epic 'Why ask to know what date, what clime?' begun in 1846 and abandoned, then restarted at an unknown later stage and finally begun again as a quite new poem in May 1848. The alterations apparent in the second part of this work seem similar to those of Emily's earlier work, and this might appear surprising. It might be thought that such thorough revision could have stemmed from the rigours of publication or from the need to revise *Wuthering Heights*. Emily's late work does show much greater attention to conventional punctuation and spelling, but other features of the poem accord well with what we have seen in earlier poetry, except perhaps that the alterations are more thorough-going. Whole sections are crossed through, and Hatfield goes beyond the poet's intention in restoring them. However, sense cannot be made of the narrative without the deleted parts, and it may appear that in 1848 when Emily came back to work she decided that, though this work had merit and was worth pursuing, there was nothing sacred about the manner in which she had set it out.

Parts of the manuscript show enormous toil on the part of the author, as though labouring intensely for the result desired. Since the design seems to have stayed in her mind for at least two years, it cannot be asserted that the conception of the poem was spontaneous. This is certainly not one of the many works where Emily Brontë begins with a state or feeling of her own fleetingly experienced and then recorded as the beginning of a Gondal poem (though we do find the harmony between the real and the dramatic date, September, which is changed in the 1848 version). It is interesting to speculate on the last line of the poem, blotted on to the opposite page when the manuscript booklet was hastily shut with the ink still very wet and immediately after another blot had been dropped from the pen. Such uncontrolled blotting does not occur on Anne's last verses!

Creative earnestness does not make an immortal poet. The examples adduced in this chapter of alterations showing Emily Brontë's technique do not unfortunately include poems of genius. Among the second copies and modifications extant there are few relating to Emily's greatest poetry, except in so far as she seems to have revised under Charlotte's influence for the 1846 edition. Such revisions cannot be regarded as typical and are in some cases perhaps better seen as preludes to the alterations of 1850, when Charlotte was able to have her own editorial way. It may be that the greatest poems were the subject of as much careful rewriting and toil as the examples adduced here. Certainly some do begin from poetic 'seeds' such as those mentioned above. Deductions about them should be made with caution, but at least the poems mentioned here may give some notions of Emily Brontë's general procedure and aims.

NOTES

1. There is an excellent reproduction of the diary paper in B. Wilks, *The Brontës* (London, 1975) p. 55.
2. E. Chitham, *The Poems of Anne Brontë* (London, 1979) pp. 71, 169.
3. The old Haworth church clock is mentioned in the article 'An American Visitor for Mr Brontë', in *BST*, vol. LXXIX (1969) p. 330. Mrs Margaret Smith has pointed out to me that there is an illustration of Haworth *old* church, including the original clock, in Whiteley Turner's *A Spring-time Saunter*, 3rd edn (1913) facing p. 94. The sister is likely to have been Charlotte, at home after her employment at Stonegappe.
4. For example H184 and some of the fragments.
5. Remarks made in this chapter about Gondal complement the general thesis maintained in the following chapter.
6. M. Spark and D. Stanford, *Emily Brontë* (London, 1959) p. 216 etc.
7. Ibid., p. 153.
8. All numbers are from C. W. Hatfield, *The Complete Poems of Emily Jane Brontë* (Oxford, 1941).
9. H. Dingle, *The Mind of Emily Brontë* (London, 1974).

5 Gondal's Queen: Saga or Myth?

EDWARD CHITHAM

There is a whole range of different stances concerning Emily Brontë's imaginary island of Gondal and the purported writings of its heroes and heroines. It seems unlikely that we shall ever arrive at a firm and conclusive view of the relation between her poetic imagination and the part of her mind which created Gondal, but an exploration of the matter is surely desirable, if only because some rash generalisations have been made and stand in need of correction.

When Emily's work was first published she and Charlotte took care to eliminate all Gondal references, and Gondal did not feature in 1846 or 1850. Nineteenth-century readers had no idea of the existence in the poet's mind of such a fiction, and the poems were presented in such a way as to avoid division into two sections derived respectively from the Gondal transcript book and the untitled book, though both were used. The first real hint of Gondal came in Shorter's *Charlotte Brontë and her Circle*, in which the diary papers of Emily and Anne revealed names of Gondal characters and places which puzzled contemporary readers.[1]

The Dodd Mead edition of 1902, though little known outside America, and the first 'complete' edition of 1910 presented readers with a tangle of unfamiliar names and initiated a fascinating detective story. M. H. Dodds made the first important contribution to the elucidation of Gondal in *MLR*, vol. XVIII (1923), but on the evidence of Hatfield's (nominally Shorter's) edition of that year she revised her ideas for a new article in *MLR*, vol. XXI (1926).[2] Commentators saw Gondal as a psychological need for Emily Brontë: typical of their comments is that of Virginia Moore, who says that, if Gondal had not symbolised her internal conflicts, it would have passed with her childhood ... [it] would have become dead for her, as it became dead for Anne, who continued to play it but in a perfunctory way, growing most indifferent just when Emily became most intense.[3]

Gondal became a major preoccupation with some commentators, especially when the Shakespeare Head Brontë, which had appeared with inaccurate texts of many Gondal poems, was supplemented in 1938 by *Gondal Poems*, edited by Brown and Mott. Among the firmest believers in its importance was Miss Fannie Ratchford of Texas, USA, whose two most definitive statements on Gondal appear in the Introduction to Hatfield's edition of 1941 and in her elaborate *Gondal's Queen*, where the poems are arranged to present 'a novel in verse', of 1955. It may here be of value to review Miss Ratchford's account of her working methods and conclusions, since they have exerted considerable influence on later writers.

By the time she came to contribute to Hatfield's edition, Miss Ratchford had studied the juvenilia of Charlotte and Branwell (in which Gondal does not appear, but which seem to have contributed to Gondal's underlying assumptions). She had spent much time trying to work out the story of Gondal from the clues provided in the poems, together with a few external references such as diary papers. She began to feel confident that she could advance a view of the Gondal story which was all-inclusive and internally consistent. On this view few poems remained unintegrated with the story. At the close of her account she says: 'Thus Emily Brontë's own voice turns into nonsense the hundreds of pages of Brontë biography based on the subjective interpretation of her poems.' But she goes on, half retracting:

> At the same time, in the poem beginning 'O thy bright eyes must answer now', she speaks in her own person, proclaiming clearly and emphatically her credo of life, the noblest apology for genius in the language.[4]

On the pages following, Miss Ratchford essays a chronological reconstruction of Gondal, a work she was to revise and complete in *Gondal's Queen*.

Miss Ratchford's argument was persuasive and the appearance of this reconstruction in a work so authoritative as that of Hatfield gave added weight to her work in the eyes of the public, especially when her study of the juvenilia of the two elder Brontës, *The Brontës' Web of Childhood*, published in 1941, showed the interest to be derived from deciphering and editing minor works of the Brontës' extreme youth. The publication of these works, especially Charlotte's, has continued in recent years and it is understandable that a parallel should be drawn between Charlotte and Emily: if Charlotte's juvenilia throw light on *Jane Eyre*, Gondal will throw light on *Wuthering Heights*. There is, however, no such exact parallel; no juvenile work of Emily or Anne has been discovered, and the remnant of Gondal that we have is not juvenilia, although it does have some bearing on Emily's novel, as Mary Visick was able to show in *The Genesis of Wuthering Heights*.[5]

In *Gondal's Queen* Miss Ratchford was able to give much space to the elucidation of her methods and the growth of her interest in Gondal. She recalls that she had been interested years before M. H. Dodds produced her article in *MLR*, and that this interest was advanced by reading the 1923 edition of Emily's poems.[6] From then on she pursued Gondal, being delighted by the discovery of Anne's list of Gondal proper names inserted in Goldsmith's *Grammar of General Geography* and the list of Gondal names appearing on a small part of MS D8, which shows that Emily, at least on this occasion, was planning her creation systematically. These discoveries showed conclusively: 'Gondal was a compact and well-integrated whole, rather than the sprawling, formless thing some would make it.'[7]

However, with all this data before her, all the initials listed and the proper names card-indexed, Miss Ratchford was puzzled by the appearance of two 'arch-heroines', one of whom is called A. G. A. and the other Rosina. She finally became convinced that 'A. G. A. and Rosina are one', though she follows this with an apparent concession as she writes: 'unless, as Miss Dodds guessed, A. G. A. is the daughter of Rosina and Julius, inheriting her mother's territorial designation'.[8] But we need not agree with Miss Dodds, for:

A. G. A. cannot be Rosina's daughter, for the *only daughter of whom we are told* is born just before or just after Julius's assassination, whereas it is evident that A. G. A. is somewhat though not greatly older than her step-daughter, Angelica, who in 'The Death of A. G. A.' identifies herself as one of the plotters of the assassination, making it clear that her motive was revenge against A. G. A. through Julius.[9] [My italics]

The weakness of the logical link here, with its underlying assumption, nowhere argued, that we have all of the Gondal story in the poems undermines the conclusion. We are not 'told' of anything to do with Gondal by Emily Brontë: we eavesdrop and hear fragments of narrative only. Dr Phyllis Bentley, generally an admirer of Miss Ratchford's work, wrote in a review:

> I own I found it difficult at first to accept that A. G. A., Geraldine and Rosina were one and the same woman. But it was a habit of the Brontës to call their daydream characters by many different names ... Miss Ratchford's evidence at last convinced me.[10]

The unity of the story told in *Gondal's Queen* is beguiling. It is possible to read the book, with its interpretations and summaries, and to feel that the author has succeeded in unravelling the complex plot of Gondal and reduced it to order. Once established, this order acquires the aura of inevitability and the reader is lulled into building further conclusions on a shaky foundation.

Remembering that Miss Ratchford was spurred in her Gondal studies by the list of characters on MS D8 and lists in Anne's handwriting, we may wish to turn to those tiny paper scraps for illumination. Anne's are disappointing, since hardly any of the names on the lists coincide with names in Emily's poems. But the D8 fragment is no better, presenting us with 'Ronald Stwart', 'Regina', 'Marcellus Stwart', 'Flora' and 'Francesca'. In the poems Regina is a place and Flora a very minor character; the others are not identifiable.[11]

A further argument against the neat story of *Gondal's Queen* lies in the author's indiscriminate use of the two transcript books of 1844. In Chapter 6 I shall maintain that the content of these booklets is quite distinct. Of the poems copied into the untitled manuscript (Hatfield's A MS) not one contains a Gondal name or signature. On the other hand the B MS, headed 'Gondal Poems' includes forty poems with Gondal signatures or headings. We have here two notebooks very different in content, which have to be considered separately.

However, in *Gondal's Queen* Miss Ratchford obscures this distinction, though she appears to have doubts about a small number of poems which prove extremely intractable to an editor convinced that Emily Brontë is all Gondal:

> In my conviction that Emily's verse, as we have it, falls within the Gondal context, I am not forgetting a small group of distinctly subjective pieces. These, more emphatically even than the narrative, reveal the dominating and directing influence of the Gondal narration in her life. They are eight in number.[12]

She then takes these eight poems, some of which are nature poems, and interprets them as poems of conflict between Emily's desire to live in this world, a world of nature and family, and the world of Gondal. However, the poems nowhere mention Gondal by name though one ('A little while') clearly does refer to it. In the main they are poems about Imagination, but there is nothing whatever to suggest that Emily is always equating Imagination with Gondal creation. On the contrary, as will be seen later, she had almost certainly adopted ideas from such Romantics as Coleridge and Shelley. So strong is the impression of her reliance on some kind of spiritual–imaginative experience totally unconnected with Gondal that many commentators have described her as a 'mystic'.[13]

The attempt to force all Emily Brontë's poetry into a Gondal context may not only be impossible: it may be misleading even in so far as it succeeds. Derek Stanford has considerable doubts about the value of a knowledge of Gondal, and though his doubts may in part stem from the influence of the 'New Critical' school, he argues convincingly that, 'what is good in Gondal is incidental and irrelevant to it, whilst what is most successfully designed as part of a whole is generally bad'.[14]

Among the clearest cases of Gondal's irrelevance is the poem which Charlotte found attractive, but so uneven that she was forced to divide it into two parts and print two sections only, leaving out the Gondal thread on which it is hung. This poem, H190, is called in the manuscript 'Julian M and A. G. Rochelle'. Stanford shows (developing a point made by Charles Morgan) that the Gondal portions of the poem are weak, 'tawdry commonplace' stanzas, and says, 'the language reveals an intermittence of power which comes and goes'.[15] A study of this poem will perhaps reinforce the view I suggest in Chapter 2 that Gondal is often brought in to help out Emily's poetic composition at the point where inspiration fails, and that the Gondal story forms part of her conscious preoccupation, while her true poetic genius often acts at a deeper level and flowers most strongly in non-Gondal poems and those parts of the Gondal poems where Gondal narrative and dramatic paraphernalia are furthest away.

We have now reached a point at which we can see that in the absence of any prose record of Gondal – and there is none whatsoever – reconstructions are likely to be tentative and full of gaps; this need have no serious bearing on the understanding of Emily Brontë's best poetry. Miss Ratchford, in her modesty, accepts that her reconstruction is not a final one, and indeed both Laura Hinckley and W. H. Paden have tried to modify her version.[16] There is no doubt that such reconstructions have had their value, even if only to show that Emily had the experience of planning a detailed plot well before the advent of *Wuthering Heights*. But we have also suggested that the attempt to subsume all her poetry into the Gondal saga can have a bad effect on its interpretation. Not only does Gondal appear to act as a patch to cover up the threadbare gaps in the inspired work, but it can also act as a will o' the wisp leading away from true understanding. It may be, in fact, that Emily, failing to comprehend the full nature of her poetic gift, interposed Gondal between her conscious self and the workings of her subconscious, so that she was able to direct composition into a secret but controlled channel and thus find expression for an artistic gift which might master her. This at any rate appears to be one strand in the argument of poem H176, 'O thy bright eyes must answer now'.

It would seem that the task of dividing Emily Brontë's poetic output into Gondal and non-Gondal elements is by no means as difficult as has been made to appear within the critical and biographical tradition of the last 40 years. Clear grounds have been mentioned above and in Chapter 4, enabling us to have confidence in her own classification when copying the poems into two booklets in 1844 and when continuing these collections by adding new poems composed during the years 1844–8. There is indeed a great overlap in style and content between the two types of poems, yet they are in the last analysis distinguishable.

Two further problems are posed. Granted that the division of works written after February 1844, and of some earlier ones, is done for us by the poet herself, we may still ask whether there is any way to classify the poems occurring only in MS C or the early fragments. Second, in considering the Gondal booklet, we may wish to know how far Emily's personal thought and feeling are reflected in these poems, and how far they are dominated by superficially invented character and event, possibly reflecting Emily's need to escape from the pressures exerted by a strong mind and will upon a bewildered young woman who was, as evidenced by her diary papers, in many ways a very ordinary domesticated person.

It has been suggested above that at times subconscious pressure invaded the Gondal narrative powerfully. Sections of the poem mentioned (H190) have often been taken as a description of the poet's own feeling when confronted with an experience thought to be 'mystical'. Derek Stanford argues that the central section of the poem, beginning 'Yet tell them, Julian, all' is an intrusion after a break which he calls 'spiritually a cleavage' between the low-keyed Gondal section and the following seven stanzas.[17] It seems that here and in other probable examples a forceful inspiration stemming from the unconscious regions of Emily Brontë's personality has broken the continuity of the Gondal fabric, presenting us with a text much superior to the surrounding pedestrian material. It may be possible to find similar eruptions among the unclassified poems of MS C or the fragments, and reference will be made to some of these in Chapter 6.

On the whole, earlier poems are harder to label than later ones, and there may be occasions when we cannot be sure whether a poem relates to Gondal or not. Some poems, as we saw previously, begin with an observation on the present scene and then 'modulate' to Gondal, sometimes to their detriment. Others exist only in small fragments, leaving it likely that Emily had failed to find a Gondal story into which she could fit the poem begun inspirationally. But there are some hints that the early copy MSS (D4–D12 and other associated fragments) classify at times; for instance the symbol 'O' occurs at the top of some poems which seem personal. It would be unwise to stress this too far, but in other MSS too Emily Brontë seems to have been a classifier; Brown and Mott mention this in *Gondal Poems* and the same tendency is noted in MS A.[18] Very probably we may take poems marked 'O' in the fragment MSS as personal, though the vast majority of the poems we have which were written before 1838 seem to be Gondal narrative (at times invaded by personal feeling).

It is because of the general difficulty of tracing external evidence bearing on the poems that considerable attention needs to be paid to such matters as contemporary weather records. However, despite Herbert Dingle's belief that these could be used to sort out Gondal from non-Gondal poems, it may appear that such a hard and fast division is impossible to draw and that ambient weather affected both Gondal and non-Gondal work.[19]

We are left, therefore, in the unclassified fragments and pages of MS C with special proper names as the main indicator of a Gondal poem. Sea, rivers, palaces, cathedrals, dungeons, mountains and deer are some other items which enter the poems and are not found in Haworth. They may indicate fiction, but they cannot be taken to prove conclusively that the poem is not concerned with the actual world of Yorkshire. 'Mountains', for example, is an unlikely word to use of the Haworth moors, but it seems that sometimes Emily is so using it, just as St Michael's Church sometimes becomes 'the minster'. On the other hand there is no point in denying that the presence of fictional characters such as Julian, Geraldine, Douglas, Gleneden and the others must indicate that the poem is part of the Gondal collection, 'sprawling and formless' or not.

Can we reconstruct Gondal more effectively than Miss Ratchford, Laura Hinckley or W. H. Paden? How far should their reconstructions be accepted? As Mary Visick shows in the comparison between Gondal and *Wuthering Heights*, there are parallels between the poems and the novel. If no reconstructions had ever been attempted, such parallels would not have come to light. The repetition of certain names in the poems and in particular the long series of poems 'signed by' A. G. A. make it tempting to try to make the references add up to a coherent story. The point made by Miss Ratchford in defence of her assertion of the oneness of Geraldine, A. G. A. and Rosina is also a fair one: the older Brontës do call their characters by several names simultaneously.[20] But we are forced to look at two inconvenient facts: the absence altogether of Gondal prose, and the incompatibility for the most part of the traces in diary papers, Anne's lists and the previously mentioned list by Emily with the names occurring in the preserved Gondal poems. This does not mean that future Gondal reconstructions are impossible, but that they must be gapped and tentative.

It is quite likely that in some senses Emily Brontë *was* A. G. A., yet the identification is far from complete and may not even be illuminating. In all likelihood the legend of 'Gondal's Queen' is only one of many sagas now lost. The evidence suggests that when a person (or persons) becomes the author for a long period of life of such totally imaginary tales in an imaginary world, he or she modifies the stories written early on by changes and additions produced later which would make nonsense of the early parts (a comparable legend in some ways is that of J. R. R. Tolkien, whose son clearly had great trouble in harmonising conflicting strands in the primitive layers of saga when he prepared *The Silmarillion* for publication).[21]

There is a danger in reconstructing that material unrelated to a given saga is attached to it merely because the reconstructor is ignorant perforce of the real background. Thus Miss Ratchford does not tell us precisely who 'Julian M' or 'A. G. Rochelle' are; they may be the same as Julius Brenzaida and A. G. A. but not even identity of name – let alone similarity – in the works of Emily Brontë guarantees identity of person: a literary investigator of the future putting together fragments of a rediscovered *Wuthering Heights* could make profound errors if he failed to distinguish Catherine from Cathy and Linton Heathcliff from Heathcliff and Edgar Linton.[22]

I conclude that a good deal of Gondal must remain a closed book and that only the most clearly defined links in the poems can be taken as incontrovertible evidence. That the feelings, feuding characters, life-crises and settings of the Gondal people can be described better than they so far have been is quite possible; but that a wholly convincing account of the web of story spun by Emily and Anne (and doubtless altered many times) can now be presented I doubt. In general, I would prefer to focus on the non-Gondal aspects of Emily Brontë's work, considering that Gondal can well become a hindrance to the understanding and interpretation of her best poems, linking them as it seems to do with Scott and Byron and drawing our attention away from her relationship with such Romantics as Coleridge and Shelley.

NOTES

1. C. K. Shorter, *Charlotte Brontë and her Circle* (London, 1896) p. 150.
2. M. Dodds, 'Gondaliand', *MLR*, vol. XVIII (1923) pp. 9–21, and 'A Second Visit to Gondaliand', *MLR*, vol. XXI (1926) pp. 373–9.
3. V. Moore, *The Life and Eager Death of Emily Brontë* (London, 1936) pp. 197–8.
4. Fannie Ratchford, *Gondal's Queen* (Austin, 1955) p. 16.
5. Mary Visick, *The Genesis of Wuthering Heights* (Hong Kong, 1958).
6. Ratchford, *Gondal's Queen*, p. 16.
7. Ibid., p. 23.
8. Ibid., p. 27.
9. Ibid., p. 27.
10. P. Bentley, 'Reconstructing the Story of Gondal', *BST*, vol. LXVI (1956) p. 34.
11. The spelling of 'Stwart' may be Emily Brontë's abbreviation.
12. Ratchford, *Gondal's Queen*, p. 32.
13. For example, Gerin, *Emily Brontë* (Oxford, 1971) Chapter 8.
14. M. Spark and D. Stanford, *Emily Brontë* (London, 1959) p. 125.
15. Ibid., pp. 128–34.
16. Discussed in F. B. Pinion, *A Brontë Companion* (London, 1975) pp. 363, 371–3.
17. Spark and Stanford, *Emily Brontë*, Chapter 2.
18. See Chapter 6.
19. See Chapter 3.
20. For example, in the case of Zamorna; see Gerin, *Charlotte Brontë* (Oxford, 1967) pp. 53ff.
21. For Tolkien's methods of work, see *The Silmarillion* (London, 1977) Foreword, pp. 7ff.
22. See T. Winnifrith, *The Brontës* (London, 1977) pp. 36–7.

6 Emily Brontë and Shelley

EDWARD CHITHAM

> The wind I hear it sighing
> With Autumn's saddest sound ...

Though the wind blowing round Haworth parsonage on 29 October 1839 was, according to Shackleton, a north-easterly, Emily's poem reminds us of Shelley's 'West Wind', the 'breath of Autumn's being'. So well known to Emily was this west wind that she considered the east 'an uninteresting wind',[1] and is able to begin poem 148 with 'Aye there it is! It wakes tonight/Sweet thoughts that will not die' without specifying the nature of 'it' until the third stanza. There follows a poem rich in Shelleyan concepts, ending in true platonic style with the soul separating from its imprisoning body:

> Thus truly when that breast is cold
> Thy prisoned soul shall rise,
> The dungeon mingle with the mould –
> The captive with the skies.

That Emily Brontë was deeply attached to Shelleyan ideas is well known. There is, however, a tendency to ascribe this to coincidence. Winifred Gerin, for example, writing in 1971 says:

A common vision informed their work even if Shelley's Platonism derived from a long study of the Greek philosophers, whilst Emily's was purely intuitive and personal. If, untaught as she was, she thought and wrote at times like Shelley, it was out of a natural sympathy.

Emily Brontë was, doubtless, not so learned as Shelley. But she was by no means as 'untaught' as this passage implies. It might perhaps be

58

argued that Shelley was indeed one of her teachers, and that his teaching struck chords in Emily's experience and personality which made it impossible for her to neglect him. It may indeed be that she had a particular interest in him.

Unfortunately, there is a considerable problem in discovering precisely how Emily may have encountered his work and personality, since there appears to have been no volume of Shelley in Keighley Mechanics' Institute Library.[2] The Keighley Library did possess a series called 'Beauties of Literature' in which the Shelley volume was published in 1832, but although there were 40 volumes in the library stockbook, only 39 titles are given, of which Shelley is not one. It is also impossible to show that Emily could have read *The Shelley Papers* issued by his friend Medwin in 1833. However, the widowed Mary Shelley's 1839–40 edition of the poems is more likely to have come Emily's way, and one is inclined to agree with John Hewish's suggestion that the *Fraser's Magazine* articles in which the forthcoming edition was discussed through 19 pages was very probably read by the Brontë family.[3]

Late 1838 and early 1839 was a period during which Emily became fervently interested in poetry, beginning then on a consistently non-Gondal output, copying poems into her first known collection and apparently endeavouring to classify.[4] The date of the first copy-booklet, MS C, is 1839, and the poems of late 1838, personal and direct in a way that previous poems had not been, follow her arrival at Law Hill and may perhaps draw their strength to some extent from the Shelley collection quoted in the *Fraser's* article. By 1839, the new edition by Mary Shelley had reached the parsonage, since Charlotte's reference to 'wild-eyed charioteers' comes from part of 'Prometheus Unbound' ten lines below where *Fraser's* extract breaks off.[5]

For many years the influence of Byron on the work of Emily Brontë has been recognised, and certainly his works and life were familiar matter at Haworth. His biographer, Moore, was another favourite among the growing Brontës, who named a place on Haworth moor after Moore's song, 'The Meeting of the Waters', and whose poems of Ireland in chains will doubtless have contributed to the mythology of Gondal civil war. Moore's *Life of Byron* included details of Shelley's romantic death in a storm, and a picture of the poet romantically portrayed and looking suitably spiritual, which was engraved by Finden from an original of Aemilia Curran. This portrait of Shelley, still the best known, attracts by its soulful expression, the dark eyes deep and moving as they stare from the pale face which surrounds them. They might well pierce the heart of young Emily Brontë as she read through the life of Byron and copied the pictures, such as the 'North Wind', originally a portrait of Byron's daughter Ianthe. Perhaps about the same time Emily and Anne read or re-read Shelley's poem on the ecstasy of love, 'Epipsychidion'.[6] Some attention now needs to be given to this poem.

'Epipsychidion' is a poem of 600 lines addressed to 'the noble and unfortunate lady, Emilia V——', in actuality Emilia Viviani, who at the age of 19 was temporarily incarcerated in a convent during parental negotiations for her marriage. Shelley acquired visiting rights to her through Claire Claremont, and it was not long before she became one more in the series of stars in his firmament, to whom he now began to apply passages from Plato's *Phaedrus* and *Symposium* and hence began to see as steps in a ladder leading from the imperfect earthly love of one individual woman to the perfect love of eternity. This background would not of course be clearly known to the Brontës, but Anne was sufficiently interested in 'Epipsychidion' and its ideas to imitate it in her poem no. 33, 'What though the sun had left my sky?'.

Shelley's poem begins by addressing Emilia as 'Sister of that orphan one' and goes on to compare her to a caged bird, 'Poor captive bird', again picked up by Anne Brontë in 'The Captive Dove'. Within three lines an analogy is being developed between the bird forgotten in its cage and a human prisoner to whose cries the 'rugged hearts' of the jailers turn a deaf ear. This motif lies near to the heart of Emily Brontë's writing, whether it stems from some actual experience of physical imprisonment, as is supposed by Romer Wilson, or because every curb on her liberty which she suffered, whether at Cowan Bridge, Roe Head, Law Hill or in Belgium, struck her as a prison. The theme of the neglected captive pervades Emily's work from 1837 (H15) in which a captive pours tears to 'wet a dungeon floor' to 1845 when 'Rochelle' can only bear prison because of her 'messenger of hope' visiting her at night.

However little Emily knew of Shelley's reasons for writing the poem, she would surely read it with breathless interest, having in mind the dark-eyed portrait from the *Life of Byron*. She could sympathise with the caged bird beating 'thine unfeeling bars with vain endeavour', as 'And like myself lone, wholly lone', shows; she would also enjoy the repeated references to the moon, a favourite of her own since at least early 1837. She would see how the poem worked at her own problems of death and eternity, the very questions which the early deaths of her mother and her sisters Maria and Elizabeth would certainly have set circling the thoughts of one who was in Charlotte's eyes 'the philosopher'. But at line 51 would come the startling assertion, bringing the attractive poet sharply before her eyes, 'Emily, I love thee'.

Lest this reconstruction of Emily Brontë's first reading of Shelley's poem may be denied, it may be as well to remind ourselves that the closeness of aspects of her poetry to Shelley have been noted by a wide range of critics and biographers from Mrs E. A. Chadwick,[7] through Derek Stanford and Muriel Spark,[8] to Winifred Gerin[9] and John Hewish;[10] that Anne imitated 'Epipsychidion' in 1844, at a time when the two sisters were especially close in poetic feeling;[11] that the speedy interest in the 1839 edition shown by Charlotte suggests some eagerness to come to grips with more of the poet's work, and that we know Emily liked to copy pictures from Finden's plates accompanying Moore's *Life of Byron*.[12]

Of course there is no knowing when Emily first came across 'Epipsychidion'; it may even have been as early as 1832–3 if the volume in the 'Beauties' series was at one time at Keighley. Let us follow Emily in her reading. Nine lines below his startling assertion of love for Emilia, Shelley talks as though he were Cathy talking to Heathcliff, 'I am not thine: I am a part of *thee*', using italics which might be recalled by Emily Brontë when she came to animate Cathy's speech to Nelly Dean. During the passage under consideration, Shelley expresses the wish that 'we two had been twins of the same mother', a notion most acceptable to Emily, whose idea of love certainly included the kind of spiritual twinship she shared at one time with Anne, and which Heathcliff and Cathy exhibit throughout *Wuthering Heights*.

'Rochelle's' messenger of Hope enters the prison 'With that clear dusk of heaven that brings the thickest stars', and the visions which he brings 'Kill me with desire'. This vision, says Rochelle-Emily, is divine, 'If it but herald Death'. In the next thirty lines of 'Epipsychidion' Shelley celebrates the way in which Emilia lured him 'towards sweet Death'; her voice murmurs so that she 'Kills the sense with passion'; her limbs are beautiful as 'the Moon/Embodied in the windless heaven of June/Amid the splendour-winged stars' (though Emily Brontë here feels it more fitting for Rochelle's vision that he 'comes with western winds', introducing an element of Shelleyan interest which he had himself omitted at that point).[13]

There are many verbal parallels between the rest of 'Epipsychidion' and Emily Brontë's work, some of which may perhaps be dismissed as chance similarities. However, if we turn from verbal similarity to similarity of ideas, the links between Shelley's poem and Emily become stronger still. For example, one major theme of *Wuthering Heights* finds its place here; the possibility of feeling love for different objects simultaneously. Cathy's marriage to Edgar Linton is often thought of as a marriage of convenience, a social step unconnected with tender feeling. This is not what Cathy herself says of it, and one may have some reservations in approving those critics who say that Cathy has betrayed her best interests and set the course of nature askew by marrying the wrong person. She tells Nelly that she loves both, and, though she differentiates between the kinds of love involved, the puzzle of her continued relations with both men is not solved by nullifying Edgar Linton's influence.

Shelley's polemic on the matter might well interest both Emily and Anne, for though he ties his view to an anti-Christian banner, which would not please the latter, a section of *Wildfell Hall* explores the problem; and Emily would have no hesitation in seconding the line 'I never was attached to that great sect . . .'. The notion that 'people hate their wives'[14] may derive from Shelley's view:

> and so
> With one chained friend, perhaps a jealous foe,
> The dreariest and the longest journey go.

Emily's religious position has sometimes been thought ambiguous, but there is a very clear statement in the non-Gondal poem H169 (non-Gondal because copied into the non-Gondal MS A):

> Was I not vexed, in these gloomy ways
> To walk unlit so long?
> Around me, wretches uttering praise,
> Or howling o'er their hopeless days,
> And each with Frenzy's tongue –
>
> A brotherhood of misery,
> With smiles as sad as sighs;
> Their madness daily maddening me,
> And turning into agony
> The Bliss before my eyes.

This diatribe does not refer to Dissenters alone, as in the case of Charlotte's attacks in *Shirley*. A typical 'wretch uttering praise' might be William Cowper, beloved of the Brontë family, who like Wesley frequently calls himself a wretch in his hymns, and who like Wesley for many years worshipped in an evangelical Anglican church, just as did the Brontë family – except Emily who apparently avoided such things and whose refusal to teach in Sunday school has been noted, and Branwell, whose opposition was more subterranean and ambivalent.

Like Shelley, Emily did not repudiate theism or the supernatural as such; far from it. She would be very pleased with his reference to the earth's 'heart':

> Awaken all its fruits and flowers, and dart
> Magnetic might into its central heart.

And she later rhymed the same two words in the last Gondal fragment:

> The wrongs that aim a venomed dart
> Through nature at the Eternal Heart.

Sea voyages are frequent in Emily's poems, and there is plenty of evidence that such books as *Gulliver's Travels* and *The Arabian Nights*, and such poems as Cowper's 'Castaway' were the Brontës' staple diet as children.[15] Shelley frequently uses a sea metaphor, and as will be seen later, his death at sea, romantically shipwrecked in a storm, may have had its effect on Emily. In the meantime, when she reached line 417 of 'Epipsychidion' she would apparently receive a direct invitation:

> Emily,
>
> A ship is floating in the harbour now,
> A wind is hovering o'er the mountain's brow;
> There is a path on the sea's azure floor,
> No keel has ever ploughed that path before;
> The halcyons brood around the foamless isles;
> The treacherous Ocean has forsworn its wiles,
> The merry mariners are bold and free;
> Say, my heart's sister, wilt thou sail with me?
> Our bark is as an albatross, whose nest
> Is a far Eden of the purple East.

In thought, Emily may have been very willing to take up the invitation.

For example, H141, 'Companions, all day long we've stood' tells of such a voyage. In the poem, the 'wild winds' are restlessly blowing. The 'shipmates' can hear 'the ocean's fall/And sullen surging swell', as they sail for 'Ula's Eden sky'. In H166 ('"Twas yesterday, at early dawn') as the snow falls 'I could not see the mountains round/But I knew by the wild wind's roar'. And thinking of Ula, 'Beyond the southern sea', the speaker recalls 'many a happy day/Spent in her Eden isle'.

The theme of justification by love so prominent in *Wuthering Heights* finds its place in 'Epipsychidion', and may in fact be regarded as one of the major components of the poem. In particular, it can extricate the captive from prison, 'a vacant prison', as Shelley says, 'this shattered prison' according to Cathy. Both writers use the notion both literally and metaphorically. Gondal characters are often detained in solid stone prisons, of which like Shelley's in 'Epipsychidion' one might say, 'The walls are high, the gates are strong, thick set/The sentinels'.[16] The prison is also a symbol for the body as in the poem already mentioned, or for the tomb where the body will lie. But love, in the case of Heathcliff and Cathy, cannot (as Shelley says):

> . . . be constrained: it overleaps all fence:
> Like lightening, with invisible violence
> Piercing its continents. . . .

So that in the end Cathy and Heathcliff will:

> . . . become the same, we shall be one
> Spirit within two frames . . .
> ·One passion in twin-hearts . . .
> One hope within two wills, one will beneath
> Two overshadowing minds, one life, one death,
> One Heaven, one Hell, one immortality.
> ('Epipsychidion', lines 583ff)

There is certainly no external evidence to show at what point Emily Brontë and her sister first came across this influential poem. Many other poems of Shelley would be interesting to them as well, and if Emily read Medwin's early accounts of Shelley's life from 1833 (she had almost ceased writing when his full biography of his friend saw the light of day in 1847) we have no positive proof of it. In these circumstances her poetic fragments of autobiography are worth examining for traces of her debt to Shelley.

It has been strongly suggested elsewhere in the present work that although the influence of Gondal on Emily's poetry is wide, there is no need to go all the way with Miss Fannie Ratchford's views on the matter. The decision to make two separate copy-books in 1844 suggests of course that Emily felt she was writing on two distinct fronts. One copy-book was clearly entitled 'Gondal Poems', and sure enough all but five of the poems in the booklet have Gondal signatures (while two of the remainder have Gondal characters named within). Equally decisively the booklet not labelled 'Gondal' contains not a single Gondal name or signature. It seems impossible to argue that no difference between the two types of poem subsisted in the mind of the author. The non-Gondal booklet need not, of course, contain only personal poems. It is conceivable that Emily had other imaginary islands or other fictional scenarios which she might have wanted to include in the non-Gondal booklet. However, an examination of Anne's poetry will show that she moved from Gondal to non-Gondal through an intermediate stage, and that when this stage was once passed, Gondal and non-Gondal poems occupied different niches in her creative life, so that the world of Gondal did not overlap into the personal poems: indeed, if anything, the personal side overlapped into the Gondal creation.[17] There is no reason why we should expect Anne and Emily to follow an identical pattern, yet the evidence is that, whereas Emily too started with wholly Gondal material (doubtless even at this stage sometimes expressing herself at a subconscious level), she gradually began to distinguish two kinds of writing (the 'O' symbols in the early copy-sheets may be an early attempt to recognise this).

By the time she moves into the 1840s, Emily at times produces poems which cannot possibly be referred to as Gondal except by a violent wrench of meaning. If we leave Gondal out of our minds, it is a worthwhile exercise to read the A poems alone. The content thus encountered gives the feel of sincerity and of personal probing. It is often allusive and obscure, but it does not give the impression as so much Gondal work does of being the tip of an iceberg of saga, known to the writer, but hampering the understanding of the reader. This is not to say of course that every incident recorded in one of the A poems must have its literal counterpart in Emily's physical life: but a poem like 'Stars', for example, seems fairly pointless if the experiences from which it is made are non-existent. In fact it needs an effort of imagination to see how such a poem can be written as an artefact with no relation to the poet's own thoughts on waking after a sleepless night watching the 'boundless regions' above, and being startled by the sun's rays. If this is not actual experience, one must postulate a secondary

Emily imagining such an experience – but with what counters to imagine? One is only likely to write about stars and their infinity, the sun and his 'hostile light' if one has felt the emotions described. Unfelt, they could not be talked of.

Poems of the A series, then, contain Emily's thoughts freed from Gondal fiction. We cannot say that everything described in them must have happened in 'real' life, but a *prima facie* case exists for considering them as in some sense autobiographical. If Emily says that the sun 'does not warm but burn', we are entitled to the belief that at some time or other this view of the sun has been her own (though the mutually contradictory opinions and feelings discoverable in the A poems make it seem unlikely that Emily always believed the same things).

Of course, these poems need interpretation. They are functioning within a poetic as well as a literal context. In H140, 'In summer's mellow midnight', we find a description of the 'cloudless moon' shining through 'Our open parlour window'. The Brontës had a parlour window which opened; the moon was full that night according to lunar calendars, and the wind ('soft' according to the poem) was blowing, according to Shackleton at strength three.[18] Emily is, as so often, beginning her poem with an observation. She continues by describing a conversation held with the night-wind. Of course it would be absurd to suppose that a person passing up Church Lane, Haworth on 11 September 1840, seeing the parlour window open, might have listened and heard two voices conversing. Plainly the conversation takes place entirely inside Emily's head, and she supplies the words which the night-wind might be supposed to speak (incidentally these include yet another 'Epipsychidion' reference in line 16, which adopts Shelley's phrase 'instinct with [spirit]' which occurs in the passage quoted above and beginning at 'We shall become the same . . . ').

Turning to a poem written earlier in the year let us try for a moment to make some sense of H134, 'Far, far away is mirth withdrawn', dated March 1840. The poem begins in a typical way, with an observation direct from life and the feeling of the moment:

> Far, far away is mirth withdrawn;
> 'Tis three long hours before the morn
> And I watch lonely, drearily:
> So come, thou shade, commune with me.

We have seen Emily 'communing' with the night-wind, and we know from that poem that she will record an imaginary conversation taking place inside her head as though it had taken place out loud, seeing herself in a poetic tradition almost as old as written poetry itself. In the present poem, she demands the presence of a certain 'shade', and we expect an imaginary conversation with, perhaps, Maria, her elder sister, whose spirit, as I shall argue in the chapter on visions, she felt to be watching her in angelic form at times, for example after waking from an 'incubus' nightmare. But we quickly find that the spirit to be entertained tonight is not Maria. It is, to begin with, a male 'shade' (final stanza), concerning whom we can build up some kind of picture as we read the poem carefully.

The shade in question was 'deserted' (5), and his corpse lies 'mingled with a foreign mould', i.e. not buried in England. Suspicions of Byron and Scott, Cowper and Swift, Brontë writer heroes, fade: all were buried in Britain. The man died 'long ago' (36) and grass has grown 'year after year' upon his grave (7). In life, he was not always honoured: we hear that he bore a 'blighted name' (9) and that the shame is 'unforgotten' (10). However, Emily will not join in his persecution: she will not join 'the mad world in all its scorn' (12). During his life the man felt 'wild despair' and she sees before her 'Thy phantom face ... dark with woe' (13). One thinks of Finden's version of the sombre Curran portrait: Shelley romanticised by sadness, in the manner of portraits of Novalis. Emily refuses to quit the sad hero, bravely saying that:

> When I hear thy foes deride
> I must cling closely to thy side.
> (19–20)

What kind of fate is predicted for the sad hero? A 'doom' 'beyond the tomb' (23–4). In other words, the man will be condemned to hell, and as we see in the next stanza, this will be for some crime committed against God, whose vengeance has thus been invoked (27–8).

It is perhaps necessary at this stage to pinch ourselves to see whether we have not totally misread the evidence and built up a picture of Emily Brontë's nightly dreaming far removed from her probable experience. This hero of whom she writes can be described negatively in many ways. He is *not* a Gondal fiction (otherwise the poem would be in the other booklet); he is famous (or infamous) enough to have roused the 'scorn' of the mad world, and therefore cannot be dismissed as some West Yorkshire exile unhappily drowned on a Caribbean voyage. He is not Byron, Scott, Cowper, Swift, Watts, Wesley, or another Brontë-approved writer or poet; he is not the Duke of Wellington (who was very much alive) nor Parry nor Ross (who did not provoke the wrath of God). He may well be the poet of the 'Epipsychidion', who wrote 'Emily, I love thee' and after leaving England in disgrace died and was buried in Italy. During his lifetime and after his death he was verbally attacked in *Blackwood's* and elsewhere, partly on the grounds of immorality, but partly because of his 'atheism' which consisted of a kind of pantheism exactly consistent with Emily's known views on such matters.

One further reference in the poem under discussion may be examined. Stanza 8 reads:

> Then do not in this night of grief
> This time of overwhelming fear,
> O do not think that God can leave,
> Forget, forsake, refuse to hear!

Two crises in Shelley's life took place during late winter. On 25 March 1811, Shelley was summoned before his tutors at Oxford to answer questions as to why he had published a pamphlet 'The Necessity of Atheism', refused to answer the questions and was expelled. However, this episode constituted disgrace rather than 'fear' and, although the circumstances might have have been unclear to Emily Brontë because of the bald account of Shelley's friend Hogg, it is difficult to see how this morning inquisition can be labelled a 'night' of fear. A year later, in 1812 (a year interesting also to Charlotte Brontë because of the Luddite riots which feature in *Shirley*) Shelley was to be found at the centre of a strange incident in North Wales. Though precise details of what happened are doubtful and may never be totally certain, Shelley claimed he had been attacked in the middle of the night of 27 February, had been shot at, and as a result had been totally unnerved. Many biographers have put this down to hallucination, but Richard Holmes, writing in 1974, regards the attack as real enough and considers Shelley's flight to Ireland on 8 March to have been a direct result. This episode might well have been described as a 'night of fear', though the date does not fit precisely with Emily Brontë's 'March'.

The poem following H134 in date is no. 13 in the A MS. It is possible that all the poems in this part of the A MS constitute a group; Emily Brontë has a strong tendency to group her poems by subject in her MSS. Even at a glance one can see that the arrangement of poems in A and B MSS is not chronological before 1844. If A 13–18 are related in subject, it may be worth extracting them from the chronological sequence and looking at them as a set. They are as follows:

A13	H135	It is too late to call thee now	April 1840
A14	H120	The wind I hear it sighing	29 Oct. 1839
A15	H121	Love is like the wild rose-briar	n.d.
A16	H122	There should be no despair for you	n.d.
A17	H123	Well some may hate and some may scorn	17 Nov. 1839
A18	H134	Far, far away is mirth withdrawn	March 1840

H121 is short and contrasts the sentiments of Love and Friendship. There are no specific references to individuals whether fictional or real. All the others in the set are longer and all enigmatic. No. 120 begins with the possibly Shelleyan reference with which this chapter began concerning the autumn wind. It develops into a mournful lament for 'Old feelings' which gather as vultures round the poet. She says she no longer has a spirit soft enough to entertain the 'fancies wild' she once cherished. These feelings will not depart, however; they have simply become 'cold and cheerless'. If they could be expelled finally, then might 'Another summer gild my cheek,/My soul, another love'.

Despite countless attempts to discover a mortal love for Emily Brontë no such person has been produced, though one can find evidence of her strong attachment to other members of her family, especially Branwell and Anne. It is of course always possible that evidence will appear, and we shall at last solve this enigma. Meanwhile it may be worth suggesting that the poet is talking here of nothing but an idolisation of Shelley, whose 'phantom face' may be the subject of A18.

The other three poems, A13, A16 and A17, are all to some extent in the first person. Not much is to be gathered from A16, which advises somebody not to despair. It may be thought that Emily is rhetorically addressing herself in this poem, and this may indeed be so. But the poem is so generalised that it is hard to see precisely what it may mean. A17 is more promising, starting as it does with an address to a man (not a woman, stanza 6) whose hopes were ruined and name blighted. In the next stanza the address is broken off, and the man is spoken of in the third person, for whom Emily no longer mourns, for 'one word' alters her opinion of him. Just possibly that word may be 'atheist' which it is said that Shelley carved 'on a Swiss Alp'. The poet now claims that the unknown man's soul is 'powerless over mine', and accuses him of vanity, weakness, falsehood and pride. There is little here to indicate any individual: indeed this could fit Shelley and many others. The poet's anger soon evaporates, as she asks herself whether she despises the timid deer for its fright, or the wolf's death howl because of its gaunt appearance. Since she does not despise these, she cannot rationally despise the dead man with the blighted hopes. This poem has at times been associated with Branwell Brontë, to whom some of the lines seem appropriate, but, though some aspects of Branwell may be in Emily's mind, the poem cannot relate primarily to him since he had still nine years to live.

In A13 Emily decides, during the month after 'Far, far away' that 'It is too late' to call her 'dream' again. The poem is a short one and concludes the series. Gone are the 'cold and cheerless' associations of A14. Instead there is a void, 'the mist is half withdrawn/The barren mountain-side lies bare', perhaps suggesting that feeling has dried up in the poet, and that she sees, with the veil withdrawn, that there is no wild 'fancy' behind it in reality. Nevertheless, the shade is a 'darling' one:

> For God alone doth know how blest
> My early years have been in thee!

It must be admitted that the reasoning process in which we have looked at Emily's enthusiasm for 'Epipsychidion', and its direct address to her, 'Emily,/A ship is floating in the harbour now', have followed this with a discussion of a group of A poems all of which may perhaps relate her confused feelings as she dwells on his picture and imagines him in conversation with herself, and have finally reached the point where she decides such fantasies cannot be entertained any longer, may well present an evidential chain that is too slight for any firm reliance to be placed on it. In these final lines, however, Emily is looking back from the age of almost 22 on an adolescent fantasy now over and done with, which has blessed her early years. That a young woman of 22 should only now be saying farewell to a romantic dream which does not differ radically from the kind of dream entertained by the twentieth-century teenager for her pop idol need not necessarily stand in the way of our acceptance of this suggestion. Whether the 'darling shade' is Shelley or not, the idol has lasted until Emily is 22, and she is only now saying goodbye to it. It must be remembered that to another dream, the world of Gondal, she never said goodbye, but was writing a new part of the story in the year of her death.

That Emily's imagination was at times unbiddable, even though firmly controlled during the writing of *Wuthering Heights*, is clear

enough. Another poem which may be partly inspired by the same
phantom, but which ends by picturing his punishment in hell, is C11
(H111) during which she may perhaps allude to Shelley's death:

> But he who slumbers there,
> His bark will strive no more
> Across the waters of despair
> To reach that glorious shore.

Under control, her imagination might have pictured God's forgive-
ness; instead she gives vent to hatred of 'the soul steeled by pride',
which 'Will never pity know' and against whom his Maker will 'mock
[the] victim's maddened prayer', while 'Revenge will reign eternally'.
Emily's hatred here is partly self-hatred, plenty of examples of which
occur in the mythologised stories of her life. Here, her imagination is
not under control, for as she says in 'O thy bright eyes' (H176), it is

> My darling pain that wounds and sears ...
> ... a king – though prudence well
> Have taught thy subject to rebel.

In such poems as H111 imagination was a 'king', controlling Emily. It
appears possible that it had controlled her sufficiently in the past to
make Shelley a personal as well as a poetic mentor, an idol of the kind
she was later to give Heathcliff, urging in 'Epipsychidion' and other
poems a kind of love and an attitude to death which find lengthy
expression on the broad canvas of *Wuthering Heights*.

There is much less to connect Emily Brontë with Coleridge than with
Shelley. F. B. Pinion notes two places in *Jane Eyre* where Charlotte
shows knowledge of 'The Ancient Mariner', and as we shall see there is
enough evidence to suggest, though not conclusively, that Emily also
found the poem attractive.[19] Some archaising of English is common to
Coleridge and other Romantics; it is impossible to say exactly where
the Brontës found words like 'methinks' and 'adown'. However, it
does seem certain that one poem of Coleridge, at any rate, penetrated
deep into Emily's mind because she found it congenial and it struck a
chord there.

Coleridge's 'Christabel' had been printed since the *Lyrical Ballads* in 1816, 1828, 1829 and 1834. It early became one of his best-known poems despite its incomplete state. It would certainly have been in the same volume from which Charlotte read 'The Ancient Mariner', and seems likely to have been read by the Brontës on numerous occasions. There can be little doubt that this is the source of the Gondal name 'Geraldine', and it seems that the name was adopted by Emily as an indication of her heroine's dubious or ambivalent nature. More controversially, I believe it probable that Emily Brontë associated the 'good and bad twin' element of the poem with herself, seeing herself as part of the Emily–Anne duo ('like twins', as Ellen Nussey said) and furthermore seeing herself as the darker, more subterranean twin, not on the side of the angels (Angelica, indeed, is one of the pair who eventually kill Geraldine in the Gondal epic). She also may have felt the irreconcilable duality within herself (in 'The Philosopher' it is an irreconcilable trinity) and one psychological function of Gondal was undoubtedly to work out the less acceptable side. (The fact that Gondal proved incapable of bearing such a burden was perhaps one reason why Emily turned to *Wuthering Heights*.)

In *The Road to Tryermaine* (Chicago, 1939) A. H. Nethercott traced the sources of 'Christabel', noting that it had already been discovered that Coleridge used a topographical work, Hutchinson's *The History of the County of Cumberland* as the source of the northern names in the poem. However, he was the first to find the name Geraldine in the same local history book. The name appears to have been Irish in origin, and to have first entered English Literature in Surrey's sonnets to Geraldine Fitzgerald, daughter of the Earl of Kildare. The name had persisted in Cumbria, where the family had close associations, and thus Coleridge came across it in the topographical work and adopted it.

However, except in reference to Surrey's beloved, the name was not in frequent use. It is unlikely that Emily Brontë obtained it from Pope's 'Windsor Forest', whereas in 'Christabel' the name was prominent and alluring. It is possible that it could have been brought more sharply before her mind in a *Blackwood's* article relating to the poem or its derivative, Martin Tupper's 'Geraldine'; such reviews occurred in 1836 and 1838.

The night scene at the start of 'Christabel' is echoed in H46 in which a 'castle bell' tolls one o'clock and H114 where 'The midnight hour/Has tolled the last note from the minster tower' (a poem, as already mentioned, in which Haworth is as present as the land of romance). The symbolic lamp of lines 184ff is the 'Signal Light' of

H190 (in Coleridge, as in Emily Brontë, the lamp is 'trimmed' by a good character for the salvation of a 'wanderer'). Geraldine stares at the air to see ghosts, just as Heathcliff does. The 'glittering' gems in Geraldine's hair, and her serpent eyes, remind us of the basilisk eyes in 'And now the housedog', as well as Heathcliff's eyes.

Christabel's 'sweet vision' (line 325 and elsewhere) of the mother, now her guardian angel, is akin to Emily's early, calming, yet disturbing vision of Maria (see Chapter 10). But Augusta Geraldine Almeda, as we understood her character from the Gondal poems, is a queen outcast, with power to make one love or fear; no one would see any connection between her and a 'sweet' vision.

'The Death of A. G. A.' (H143), of which the first part dates from January 1841, uses syntax and verse form akin to 'The Ancient Mariner'. There is, for example, the use of 'as' = 'as if, as though' in line 15, comparable to line 166 of 'The Ancient Mariner', 'As they were drinking all'. Angelic spirits are a powerful feature in 'The Ancient Mariner' and perhaps find an echo in lines 45–8 of 'The Death of A. G. A.' where 'that holy sky' is also reminiscent of 'Christabel'. In line 83 we find Angelica describing Geraldine's decisive act in this way:

> With her own hand she bent the bow
> That laid my best affections low.

Angelica gives the history of her childhood love for Geraldine and enlarges on her early treacheries:

> She was my all-sufficing light,
> My childhood mate, my girlhood's guide,
> My only blessing, only pride.

The 'childhood twin' motif here is a reflection of the real situation between Emily and Anne and a forerunner of that between Cathy and Heathcliff. The 'united but contrary' twins produce the same kind of numinous shudder as the 'twain' who cast lots in the phantom boat seen by the mariner.

There may also be a reflection of 'The Ancient Mariner' in a poem that Robin Grove considers 'Emily Brontë's best poem', 'Stars' (H184).[20] Here the sun rises menacingly after a night of cool:

> Blood-red he rose, and arrow-straight
> His fierce beams struck my brow.

The heat generated by the sun in the poem is the same intense and inimical heat as that of the sultry sun in 'The Ancient Mariner', lines 111ff.

How much Emily Brontë knew of Coleridge's thought on the nature of Imagination it would be difficult to say. *Biographia Literaria* does not seem to have been in Keighley Mechanics' Institute Library, though an edition of *Table Talk*, probably that edited by H. N. C. Coleridge and first published in 1834, does appear. From this she might just have obtained the stimulus for 'Love and Friendship', since Coleridge is recorded as having commented on the distinction between them on 27 September 1830.[21] The distinction, however, is a sufficiently perplexing one to have been in Emily's thoughts without reading Coleridge.

Both Fancy and Imagination are referred to in poems of 1844, and in 'A Day Dream' (H170), though it is very Shelleyan she describes the dream as a 'reverie', the word Coleridge uses in the introductory notes to 'Kubla Khan'. In line 43 of the same poem she declares,

> A thousand thousand silvery lyres
> Resounded far and near,

both the phrase and the rhythm reminding us of 'The Ancient Mariner', lines 238–9,

> And a thousand thousand slimy things
> Lived on; and so did I.

The 'Fancy' here referred to by Emily Brontë, the air above bursting into fire, is the same as the mariner sees:

> The upper air burst into life!
> And a hundred fire-flags sheen,
> To and fro they were hurried about!

Six days after this, Emily wrote one of her 'sea voyage' poems, using the ballad metre of 'The Ancient Mariner' (H171), in which there are many verbal similarities with Coleridge, though the poem is not in Emily's best manner. In September, she is discussing 'Fancy' in a poem called 'To Imagination'. In this poem, Reason stands against Imagination, which she calls 'benignant power' and seems to suggest (stanza 5) is an 'intimation of immortality' which affords a glimpse to the 'real' world beyond the grave. However, if she had read and understood the passage in which Coleridge makes his well-known pronouncement on the distinction between two types of Imagination and Fancy, there is no indication of this in her poems, and in fact she seems to obscure the difference in the present poem; though paradoxically the content of such a poem as 'A Day Dream' compared with 'The Philosopher', seems almost to exemplify Coleridge's distinction.

It is in this last-mentioned work that Emily seems to derive most from the underlying tone of both Shelley and Coleridge. Kubla Khan's 'sunless' sea has here become an 'inky' sea, and the archetypal mariner a prophet. As in Shelley and 'The Ancient Mariner' the 'Spirit' is no light fancy, but a burning and intense representation of a facet of Emily's subconscious understanding. By 1845, her reading of these major Romantics had so far permeated her creative personality that she found it perfectly natural to talk in their language, and explore through language a personal situation which, despite her reliance on the ideas and poetic forms of the previous generation of poets, was hers alone and could only be solved by her own creative genius.

NOTES

1. Letter from Anne Brontë to Ellen Nussey, 4 October 1847.
2. C. Whone, 'Where the Brontës Borrowed Books', *BST*, vol. LX (1950) pp. 344–58.
3. J. Hewish, *Emily Brontë* (London, 1969) p. 146. Ponden Hall may also have been a source here.
4. D group of MSS, mostly at BPM.
5. W. Gerin, *Emily Brontë* (Oxford, 1971) p. 153.
6. Gerin, in *Emily Brontë*, begins to explore this possibility.
7. E. Chadwick, *In the Footsteps of the Brontës* (London, 1914).
8. M. Spark and D. Stanford, *Emily Brontë* (London, 1959) p. 165.
9. Gerin, *Emily Brontë*.
10. Hewish, *Emily Brontë*, pp. 34, 59, 80, 88–9, 95.
11. E. Chitham, *The Poems of Anne Brontë* (London, 1979) p. 181 etc.
12. Gerin, *Emily Brontë*, p. 44.
13. H190.
14. *Wuthering Heights*, Chapter 23.
15. W. Gerin, *Charlotte Brontë* (Oxford, 1967) pp. 24ff.
16. 'Epipsychidion', lines 405ff.
17. The self-identification with Gondal figures such as Geraldine appears to be strong.
18. The precise values to be accorded to Shackleton's wind-strengths is uncertain, but three appears to be relatively high in his scale.

19. For example in H95. Branwell too appears to have read and been impressed by the poem.
20. R. Grove, 'It Would Not Do: Emily Brontë as Poet', in A. Smith (ed.), *The Art of Emily Brontë* (London, 1976).
21. S. Coleridge, *Table Talk* (London, 1834) p. 116.

7 Branwell Brontë and Ponden Hall

TOM WINNIFRITH

The investigation of the Brontës' literary ancestry is a dangerous business. It is easy to become obsessed with a resemblance that is trivial or coincidental. *Wuthering Heights* is one of the most original novels in the English language, but if one added up all the supposed models for this novel, one would have to believe that Emily Brontë had not an original thought in her life. Shakespeare, Hoffman, George Sand, Dickens, Walter Scott, *Blackwood's Magazine*, Yorkshire gossip and Irish family history are all supposed to have made their mark, and perhaps some of them had some influence. Influences on Charlotte are perhaps a little easier to track down. We do know a little more about what Charlotte had read (and had not read), and a clear autobiographical line is marked, whereas we know little about Emily's life and less about her reading. Even with Charlotte the autobiographical and literary influence is a great deal more subtle than most biographers and literary historians have assumed. With Anne and Branwell, less impressive writers than Charlotte and Emily, literary sources are less likely to be filtered and refined. Since Anne was almost always fairly close to Emily and Branwell often fairly close to Charlotte, we can learn something about possible literary influences on the two greatest Brontës from studying the works of their less well known brother and sister.

In editing Branwell's poetry I was struck by a number of lines which appear to be fairly direct imitations of a number of English poets. Before accusing Branwell of plagiarism it would be as well to remember that there was nothing particularly wicked or foolish in adapting a poem by Byron to the situation of Angria if Branwell's adaptation was not intended for publication. Branwell's *Misery* poems, sent first to *Blackwood's* and then to Wordsworth, do contain reminiscences of Wordsworth and Coleridge. This was perhaps tactless in view of the fact the child who is father to the man in the *Misery* poems is such an obvious villain. Sub-Wordsworthian and pseudo-Byronic poems were no doubt written and printed all over England in the middle of the nineteenth century, and we should admire, not condemn, Branwell for providing us with some of the better specimens of this genre. It is perhaps worth mentioning that Branwell, unlike his sisters, had received some sort of classical education. This would certainly have entailed the study of Latin authors who modelled themselves on Greek originals without any accusations of plagiarism or parody. It might possibly have included the writing of Latin and Greek compositions in which the student was supposed to model himself on the style of a classical author.

We do not know much about Branwell's education. Charlotte's letters and hints in her novels give us some indication of the careful but stilted way in which she was educated, and we know that her sisters, albeit falteringly, followed in her footsteps. But Branwell's education at home under his father's tuition is something of a mystery. It included the Classics, but we do not know how good at the Classics Mr Brontë was, or how good Branwell became. It would seem probable that, free from the routine of school and free from a routine of domestic tasks which even in the liberated twentieth century are more likely to fall to daughters than to sons, Branwell had ample opportunity to read on his own, and it was this reading that explained his reputation for precocity.

Nor can there be much doubt where Branwell did his reading. The Heatons of Ponden Hall obviously had a part to play in the Brontë story, and this part has not been fully explained.[1] Dark hints of romantic involvements between Brontës and Heatons, still lingering in Haworth folklore, may safely be ignored, although a resemblance between Ponden Hall and Thrushcross Grange, a link between the story of *Wuthering Heights* and episodes in Heaton family history, and even the name Heaton as a source for Hareton and Heathcliff are more promising sources of enquiry. More prosaically and more certainly the library at Ponden Hall would seem to be the place where the young Brontës, particularly Branwell, did much of their adolescent reading.

In Victorian novels of the sub-Trollopian variety the rector and the squire together with their families have an easy affinity with each other, sharing common social obligations and enjoying a common education. Mr Brontë was not quite the ordinary Victorian clergyman, and the Heatons were certainly not ordinary Victorian squires. Nevertheless, the Brontës and Heatons were bound to maintain contact with each other, and it is certain that one result of this contact was that the Brontës were allowed a free run of the magnificent Ponden Hall library.

The catalogue of this library has not been published, although it can easily be consulted in the Haworth Parsonage Museum. The library was sold by auction on 4 November 1899 by Mr William Weathered. There were 1355 lots in the sale, and the catalogue, though it is not without misprints and is assembled in rather a haphazard fashion, gives a fair indication of the flavour of the library. Although the Heatons were an old family and many of the books date back as far as the seventeenth century, most of them would seem to have been bought at the end of the eighteenth century by Robert Heaton, who was born in 1726 and died in 1794, grandfather of the squire, also called Robert Heaton, who was in residence for most of the Brontës' lifetime, dying in 1846. It is not clear why the elder Robert should have suddenly decided to amass this library, although more books were bought by later Heatons, and his greatgrandchildren, the younger contemporaries of the Brontës, had literary and musical tastes, as is shown by their copying out poetry in commonplace books and composing music.

Proof that the Brontës used the library is not hard to find. Winifred Gerin has already pointed out[2] that one of Branwell Brontë's early manuscripts is modelled on Chateaubriand's *Travels* of which there was a copy in the Ponden Hall library; Branwell and this catalogue (lot no. 1273) both make the mistake of giving Chateaubriand's particule a capital D. Gerin also points out the presence of Mungo Park's *Travels* in the library (lot no. 1303) as a source for the Brontës' knowledge of Africa; lot 228, *Proceedings of the Association for Discovering the Interior Parts of Africa* (2 vols, 1810) looks interesting. Beaumont and Fletcher's *Salmosis and Hermaphroditus*, first printed in 1602, is described in the catalogue (lot no. 71) as 'Beaumont, Fletcher, *Hermaphrodite* (title-page gone, very old)' and is thought to be the origin of the odd phrase 'whey faced hermaphrodite', improbably used by the young Brontës. This is perhaps a less certain link, but given the stronger pieces of evidence we can amass a multiplicity of other connections between the Ponden Hall library and the reading of the Brontës.

Mr Brontë made notes from Buchan's *Domestic Medicine*; this is lot no. 397 in the library. Thomas Bewick was a strong influence on Charlotte as a painter, and illustrations by Bewick are a feature of a number of the books catalogued, as, for example, lot 855 *Poems* by the Rev. Joseph Relph, which was published in 1798 and embellished with picturesque engravings on wood by Mr T. Bewick of Newcastle. Charlotte's early poem 'The Poetaster' has been shown by Melodie Monahan to be a precocious effort involving a certain knowledge of Jonson, Dekker and possibly Rymer as well.[3] This must have been inspired by Ponden Hall where there is more than one copy of Jonson's work in lots 117, 464, 553 and 1140, Rymer in lot 565, and Dekker probably in the lots not very helpfully catalogued as plays (lots 97, 98 and 108–10).

In *The Brontës and their Background* I drew attention to the Ponden Hall library as a possible source of the note of licentious coarseness in the Brontës' fiction which so shocked contemporary reviewers. An eighteenth-century library was hardly suitable for a nineteenth-century reader. Plays by Wycherley (lot 113) and Aphra Behn (lots 102 and 132) would naturally be considered shocking. In the section entitled miscellaneous we find a number of tempting titles. This lot 415 is entitled *Trials for Adultery or History of Divorces*, and the full title of this work in seven volumes, published in 1799 is *Trials for Adultery, Fornication, Cruelty, Impotence and History of Divorces* (lot 461). *Nocturnal Revels* is a pornographic description of the activities of Sir Francis Dashwood. Ned Ward, the author of *Comforts of Matrimony* and *Lycidus or the Lover in Fashion* (lots 582 and 583) and the translator of *Don Quixote* (lots 528 and 578), was a noted bawdy writer.

It being established that the Brontës used the Ponden Hall library, we may look more closely at the largest section of the library, which is entitled 'Poetry' and includes lot 781 to 1263. It is difficult to do justice to this impressive collection which goes back as far as Dunbar (lot no. 797) and forward as far as Burns (lot no. 1176), but principally covers the period from 1660 to 1760, which somewhat inaccurately we entitle Augustan or eighteenth-century poetry. The absence of Romantic poetry, and even of pre-Romantic poets like Gray and Collins is presumably to be explained by the later Heatons keeping their copies of these poets for their own use, and, as will be shown later, the Brontës certainly read the Romantics. But even if the Romantics had featured at Ponden Hall they would have been outnumbered by the vast bulk of eighteenth-century poets.

The modern student of eighteenth-century poetry would recognise in the catalogue some familiar names like Pope and Dryden, Johnson and Thomson, but these are swamped by a mass of less familiar names, which only appear in literary histories if they appear at all. It is true that Charlotte in a famous letter to Ellen Nussey (written on 1 July 1834) advises her only to read the best, namely Milton, Shakespeare, Thomson, Goldsmith, Pope, Scott, Byron, Campbell, Wordsworth and Southey, but this was after some prim Roe Head education, and Ellen Nussey's taste in poetry is unlikely to have been very catholic. On their own the Brontës, and particularly Branwell, are likely to have read widely and wildly, and in writing poetry to have been influenced by the Ponden Hall library.

Among the works that may have helped the Brontës as writers of poetry were some now forgotten manuals. Thus there are no fewer than three copies of Edward Bysshe's *The Art of Poetry* (lots 952, 1000 and 1209). The full title of this work is *Rules for Making Verses: A Collection of the most natural, agreeable and sublime Thoughts on Allusions, Similes, Descriptions and Characters of persons and things that are to be found in the best English poets.* This was printed in 1718, and in 1737 a dictionary of rhymes was added. Lot 719 in two volumes is the *English Parnassus* of Joshua Poole, printed in 1677. The sub-title of this is *A help to English poesie containing a collection of all the Rythming monosyllables, the choicest epithets and phrases with some general forms upon all occasions, subjects and themes. Alphabetically digested.* The Brontës' poetry may not always be natural, agreeable, or sublime, but they certainly knew how to rhyme, and indeed in some of Branwell's poems rhyme seems to take over from reason.

Another patent influence from Ponden Hall may have been the considerable number of inferior epic poems. The world of Gondal and of Angria is close to that of the epic, sharing the same loose structure and similar larger than life heroes and heroines seeking glory through deeds gory. Of course it is a mistake to look in Gondal or Angria for the larger epic vision that distinguishes the great epic poems of Homer, Virgil and Milton. But equally it is impossible to find any real epic vision, as opposed to superficial epic trappings, in the inferior seventeenth- and eighteenth-century writers of epic poems. Among such poets in the Ponden Hall library we may notice John Harvey, author of the *Bruciad*, printed according to the catalogue in 1769 (lot 870), Richard Glover, author of *Leonidas*, printed in 1770 (lots 905 and 918), William Wilkie, author of the *Epigoniad*, printed in 1769 (lot 983), and the famous or infamous Sir Richard Blackmore, author of *Prince Arthur*, printed in 1714 (lot 1137), *Eliza*, printed in 1721 (lot 1153) and *Alfred*, printed in 1723 (lot 1163).[4] Branwell certainly imitated Glover in his three poems on the subject of Thermopylae,[5] and Bruce he cites as an example, which he alas did not follow, of triumph over adversity. Tasso is another example[6] and translations of

Tasso figure in the library (lots 503 and 1182). Ossian features prominently (lots 858, 946, 1011 and 1243). There are works on epic theory in lots 888, 925, 1024 and 1212, as well as translations from Homer, Virgil and Lucan (lots 945, 1009, 1079, 1118, 1121 and 1126).

It is sometimes difficult to distinguish bogus epics like those of Ossian or bad epics like those of Blackmore from the deservedly more famous mock epics of Pope and Dryden. There was a fair amount of mock epic in the Ponden Hall library. We may note lot 984, *The Scribleriad* by R. Owen printed in 1751, and lot 1047, *The Diaboliad* by W. Coombe printed in 1777.[7] In addition, the library contains a great deal of straightforward satire, including not only Pope, Swift, Dryden and Johnson, but more obscure satirists like Hall (lot 1040) and Oldham (lots 796, 851, 939 and 1095). Critics have noted a coarse, savage note of satire in the Brontës' mature novels, and it is certainly present in their juvenile work, especially in the writing of Branwell. It is also true that in Angria, though not in Gondal, there is slightly uneasy tension between the epic and the mock epic elements: there are times when one feels that the Brontës are mocking themselves, or, one might more unkindly suggest, each other for taking the whole business of their imaginary world so seriously.

Some eager research student could do worse than devote some of his time to noting more direct links, as opposed to general resemblances, between some of the obscure authors noted in the Ponden Hall catalogue and the fairly obscure poetry of Charlotte and Branwell. In editing Branwell's poetry I only noted the more obvious resemblances to better known poems by Wordsworth and Byron, and to add a slightly different note the hymns of Isaac Watts. Of these authors only Watts appears in the Ponden Hall library and that in an edition printed after the Brontës' death. The links between Emily's poetry and other Romantic poems which Mr Chitham suggests indicate either that the Brontës did some of their reading outside Ponden Hall, or that the owners of Ponden Hall did not include their copies of Romantic poets in the 1899 sale, and there is nothing surprising about either conclusion. But the Brontës did have access to, and Branwell at any rate used, poetry from an earlier era. Indeed one could go further and suggest that one of the reasons why much of the poetry of the Brontës is so bad is that they were too dependent upon models from a previous era as well as their own; this contrasts with the novels where with no real models upon which to draw the Brontës could show their originality, although even this originality may have been ultimately inspired by some of the obscure works recorded in the dusty catalogue of the Ponden Hall library.

NOTES

1. Mrs Mary Butterfield has printed a short pamphlet, *The Heatons of Ponden Hall* (Keighley, 1976) and is planning a longer work on the same subject. I am very grateful to Mrs Butterfield for information about the Heatons and for doing valuable preliminary work on their library.
2. W. Gerin, *Branwell Brontë* (London, 1961) pp. 43–4. Miss Gerin says that there was a copy of Voltaire's *Henriade* in the library, a work which Charlotte translated, and another indication of the interest of the Brontës in the epic, but I have not been able to find this in the catalogue.
3. M. Monahan, 'Charlotte Brontë's *The Poetaster*: Text and Notes', *Studies in Romanticism*, vol. XX (winter 1981) pp. 475–96.
4. Most of these epics are discussed by P. Hagin, *The Epic Hero and the Decline of the Epic Tradition* (Bern, 1964). Hagin mentions an epic, *Britannia*, 1801, by J. Ogilvie, and works by Ogilvie are in the Ponden Hall catalogue (lot no. 1180), although the date in the catalogue would suggest not *Britannia*, but the earlier *Rona* or *Fane of the Druids*, of 1784 and 1789 respectively.
5. Only one of these is printed in *SHCBP*, pp. 257–63, with the resemblance to Glover noted.
6. *SHCBP*, p. 388.
7. Also lots 840 and 1226 mention poems by S. Garth which almost certainly would include *The Dispensary*.

8 *Wuthering Heights*: One Volume or Two?

TOM WINNIFRITH

On 6 April 1846 Charlotte Brontë wrote to Aylott and Jones. The letter begins:

> Gentlemen – C. E. & A. Bell are now preparing for the press a work of fiction, consisting of three distinct and unconnected tales which may be published either together as a work of 3 vols. of the ordinary novel size, or separately as single vols. as shall be deemed most advisable.[1]

On 4 July 1846 she wrote to Henry Colburn in very much the same strain:

> Sir,
>   I request permission to send for your inspection the M.S. of a work of fiction in 3 vols. – it consists of 3 tales, each occupying a volume and capable of being published together or separately, as thought most advisable.[2]

We know from Charlotte's biographical notice[3] of Acton and Ellis Bell that these three tales were *Wuthering Heights, Agnes Grey* and *The Professor*. According to this same notice Anne's novel and Emily's were sent round various publishers for a year and a half, but this must be an exaggeration, since Charlotte in her letter to W. S. Williams of 17 November 1847, complaining of Newby's procrastination, says that the first proof sheets of her sisters' novels were already in the press at the beginning of August.[4] A year and a half would appear to be the time that elapsed between the completion of *Wuthering Heights* and *Agnes Grey* and their eventual publications in December 1847.

84

In the standard Haworth edition of the Brontë novels *Wuthering Heights* occupies 350 pages, *Agnes Grey* 202, and *The Professor* 269. *The Professor* was probably lengthened in one or more of the revisions that were made in it between its rejection by Smith, Elder & Co. and its posthumous publication. In the original Newby edition of *Wuthering Heights* the long paragraphs of most standard editions are broken up, and thus in this edition the second volume of *Wuthering Heights* is actually longer than the whole of *Agnes Grey*, having 209 leaves as opposed to *Agnes Grey*'s 183, and the first volume's 175.[5] In the standard Haworth edition *Jane Eyre* occupies 555 pages, *The Tenant of Wildfell Hall* 502, *Shirley* 666 and *Villette* 594.

These figures underline our instinctive feeling that whereas *Agnes Grey* and *The Professor* are makeweight novels, *Wuthering Heights* is a complete novel. This makes it very odd that the sisters originally intended to publish all three novels together, especially as the total length of the three novels (821 pages in the Haworth edition) is so much longer than any other Brontë novel. Obviously there could be some variety in the standard length of a three-volume novel and variations in the length of a single volume.[6] But though the Brontës were curiously naïve in some literary matters they, or rather Charlotte, did seem to have a very clear idea of what constituted a volume when they wrote to Aylott and Jones and Colburn, and later when Charlotte was asked to submit a three-volume novel to Smith, Elder & Co. she sent *Jane Eyre* which is 266 pages shorter than the combined length of *Wuthering Heights*, *The Professor* and *Agnes Grey*. The total length of the three-volume novel, originally proposed to publishers in 1846 is, however, less surprising than the fact that one of these novels in its original short paragraphed form, is almost as long as the other two put together.

Of course the girls were each independent. Anne and Charlotte, recognising Emily's superior merit and afraid of interfering with her, could have accepted the length of *Wuthering Heights* as a necessary inconvenience. The story of the publication of the poems is evidence of these rather frightened reactions by Emily's sisters. It would then perhaps be up to one of the publishers to whom the three tales were submitted to suggest that *Wuthering Heights* only needed one other volume to meet the requirements of a three-volume novel. This is a plausible explanation, although one might have thought that Charlotte would have said something about this change of plan, and we hear nothing about advice from other publishers, only curtly phrased letters of rejection.

There is another hypothesis which has the merit of explaining why Charlotte said nothing about the separation of *The Professor* from *Agnes Grey* and *Wuthering Heights*, and also explaining why Emily appears to have written no poetry between September 1846 and May 1848 when she made two separate drafts of a Gondal poem. Charlotte may have decided to submit *The Professor* on its own and left Emily and Anne with two volumes which needed expanding. Alternatively the decision may have been Emily's and Anne's; perhaps they were influenced by a publisher who saw more merit in *Wuthering Heights* than in *The Professor*. It is conceivable that the autobiographical nature of *The Professor* which Mrs Gaskell found so embarrassing may have contributed to the decision to split up the novels. It was possible to publish a one-volume novel, and possible to publish three volumes, each containing a different novel, but a two-volume work with each volume consisting of a separate tale was neither chalk nor cheese, and therefore at some time between July 1846 and July 1847, Emily, abandoning her poetry may have set to and composed a second volume of *Wuthering Heights*, expanding the original one volume of 200 or so pages to the length we now have. Charlotte would not mention this, or indeed say anything about the separate publications. The decision to let *The Professor* go on its own must have been one that involved considerable heart searching, if not acrimony, and Charlotte would hardly want to bring this up, especially so recently after the death of her sisters. Whichever sister had made the decision it was one which brought Charlotte eventually to the safe haven of Smith, Elder & Co., while her sisters were forced into the hands of the incompetent and dishonest Newby, and Charlotte must have felt some guilt about this.

It is possible that we have some slight indication of the time when *The Professor* was first separated from *Agnes Grey* and *Wuthering Heights*. George Smith in his memoir of 1900[7] noted that when *The Professor* first arrived at Smith, Elder & Co., the envelope had the names of three or four other publishers on it. We also know that *The Professor* was refused six times before it came to Smith, Elder & Co.[8] Presumably an envelope with three novels in it would be a different size from one with one novel, and there might be here a pointer to *The Professor* going to two or three publishers together with Anne's and Emily's works. This would suggest a date late in 1846 for the decision to split up the novels, and interestingly this is just the time when Emily appears to have abandoned writing poetry. Other reasons have been given for this abandonment: ill health and the problem of Branwell explain the failure to write in 1848, but the absence of any poetry in

1847 and late 1846 is more peculiar. Emily may have been shocked by the discovery of her poems by Charlotte, but she was willing for the poems to be published, and she did write some poetry after 1845. In the first half of 1846 she was busy with completing *Wuthering Heights* as it was first sent out to the publishers, and in the second half of 1846 and early 1847 she would have plenty of time to write a second volume. This was the time when Charlotte was engaged on *Jane Eyre* and Anne had probably started on *The Tenant of Wildfell Hall*. Both novels owe something to *Wuthering Heights*, and we have a certain amount of not very reliable evidence, sometimes adduced when trying to prove that Emily wrote a second novel, to show that Emily was writing in collaboration with her sisters during this period.[9]

The hypothesis that Emily originally wrote a one-volume novel and later expanded it to its present length has never been put forward before in spite of the vast amount of critical and biographical work on the Brontës. It involves a slightly different view of the Brontës' relations with each other than that put forward by most biographers following Mrs Gaskell's account inspired by Charlotte's recollections of her recently dead sisters. It is likely that three imaginative girls confined to each other's company and engaged on literary exercises that must have strained their capacity for cooperation would have had occasional altercations, and indeed we hear of Emily's anger on the discovery of her poems. It is possible that there was another quarrel about the first three novels and that *Wuthering Heights* was expanded because of this quarrel, but of course if Charlotte could tell us nothing about the quarrel, she would tell us nothing about the expansion.

An over-protective veneration of the sanctity of the Brontë family life is understandable. Less understandable, but just as conspicuous among Brontë students is the romantic feeling that *Wuthering Heights* is a complete work of art in itself, and as such must have sprung fully fledged from Emily's head. *Wuthering Heights* is a romantic novel and this romantic view of its inspiration and creation might have some validity, were we not aware that the creative process of writing other great novels like *Anna Karenina* and *Middlemarch*, both of which started from small beginnings, was such that we cannot assume that Emily must have had the whole plot of *Wuthering Heights* in her head when she started writing.

The third reason why nobody has put forward the theory of a one-volume *Wuthering Heights* is the most convincing. It is very difficult to work out how the novel could have existed in a shorter form. Oddly enough both *Agnes Grey* with the easily detachable

Bloomfield section and *The Professor* with its easily detachable Yorkshire chapters, some of which were probably added at a later date,
would be much easier to cut down. *Jane Eyre* is an episodic novel, *The
Tenant of Wildfell Hall* could be reduced to Helen Huntingdon's diary,
Shirley, the longest of the novels, has much superfluous padding, and
only *Villette*, in many ways the most like *Wuthering Heights* of the
Brontë novels, seems to have that kind of organic unity which means
that if we cut out one part of the work we seem to lose the whole
meaning of the novel. Interestingly *Villette* was the Brontë novel which
took longest to write.

   A starting point for trying to cut down *Wuthering Heights* into
one-volume size must be the existing division into two volumes. Not
many editions reproduce this division, and it comes as something of a
surprise to find that it takes place not after Chapter XV with the death
of Catherine, nor after Chapter XVI with her funeral, nor after Chapter
XVII with the death of Hindley just before what is virtually a twelve-
year gap in the narrative, but after Chapter XIV where Nelly stops her
narrative because the doctor has arrived allowing Lockwood to utter a
few vapid thoughts. Thus the first volume is rather shorter than the
second, and we end the first volume with the action in full swing and
nothing resolved. This not very efficient division of the volumes might
be a pointer to an expansion of *Wuthering Heights*, although it could
also point to a one-volume novel being artificially divided into two. We
cannot of course make either volume as it stands the original one-
volume novel, as so many loose ends are left unresolved, but it is worth
pointing out that there are parallels between these two volumes. In the
first three chapters of Volume I we have Lockwood's story before
getting down to the story of the elder Catherine, whereas in the first
three chapters of Volume II we have the tying up of the story of the
elder Catherine and indeed the whole of the elder generation apart
from Heathcliff, as Hindley dies and the deaths of Isabella and Edgar
are foretold.

   The two most obvious ways to cut down the novel to one-volume
size are to cut one narrator and to cut out one generation. It is part of
the charm of *Wuthering Heights* that the real world of the moors comes
through the filter of Lockwood's bogus sophistication, but it is worth
pointing out how very different Lockwood is from the other characters. The claim by Branwell's acquaintances that *Wuthering Heights*
was his work has been relegated to the wilder shores of Brontë
speculation on the grounds that Branwell's extant writings show he
could never have written anything so good, and that Emily was too

honest to pass off her brother's work as her own.[10] The former argument is a weak one in view of the poor quality of Charlotte's juvenilia, and the latter argument would be weakened if Emily had not borrowed her brother's work wholesale, but merely taken a character from it. Lockwood's false air of worldly wisdom does rather remind us of the pseudo-cynicism of Branwell himself, whose reading of the novel alleged to be the archetype of *Wuthering Heights* did not get very far. If we did remove Lockwood's presence entirely we would only remove five chapters from the novel, where he is the narrator and the equivalent of a further one chapter consisting of scattered interjections in Nelly Dean's narrative, and so, if Emily did borrow Lockwood from Branwell, or think of Lockwood by herself at some late stage, she must have found additional material for a second volume.

Other characters in the novel both serve an essential part, so that without them *Wuthering Heights* seems to fall to pieces, and yet do not occupy enough space to make a one-volume novel possible without them. Hindley plays an essential part as the cause of Heathcliff's savagery, and Isabella and her son are instruments in the working out of his vindictive plan, and yet each of these characters is really only on the stage for about eight chapters. Joseph's sour gloom pervades the moral atmosphere of *Wuthering Heights*, but the removal of Joseph would subtract little from the length of *Wuthering Heights*.

The most likely candidate for removal is the second generation. It is interesting that few films of the book have been really able to cope with the second half of the book, in which the younger Catherine, a slightly gentler and less interesting version of her mother, is matched by two lovers who in a way parallel, though in another way they parody, Heathcliff and Edgar Linton with the added subtlety that Hareton, the character like Heathcliff, is the son of Heathcliff's enemy, Hindley, while the character like Edgar Linton is the son of Heathcliff himself. The subtlety and the fact that the second generation show the success and ultimate failure of Heathcliff's plan for vengeance may seem an essential part of *Wuthering Heights*, in the same way as Lockwood's dream and the final ambiguous chapter seem essential, difficult though it is to interpret either satisfactorily. But we can imagine a novel that started off in Chapter IV with the words 'One fine summer morning'. Nelly Dean's position both as nursemaid and omniscient narrator is made fairly clear in this exciting chapter, and Lockwood's presence, of which we are reminded in occasional intervening chapters, could be fairly easily removed.

We would then have reduced *Wuthering Heights* to the simple, yet touching, love story between Heathcliff and Catherine. Obviously this would be a less rich if less complicated novel, operating more on the Romantic than the metaphysical plane. We would lose very fine scenes such as Lockwood's dream and the account of Heathcliff's death. Unlike Coleridge's wedding guest Lockwood does not leave us a sadder and a wiser man, and we feel that this failure of Lockwood to comprehend is part of Emily's message. It is possible, however, that something might be gained from reducing the novel. The love affair, if one can call it that, between Linton Heathcliff and the younger Cathy, has always seemed unreal and unlikely, and Heathcliff's villainy in encouraging this love affair is in a way inconsistent with the more sympathetic treatment of Heathcliff in the earlier part of the narrative. Hareton is a more interesting character, but the final courtship of Hareton and Cathy and their move to Thrushcross Grange is at once both puzzling and a little tame. A one-volume *Wuthering Heights* would be a slighter but more coherent work than the novel we have.

NOTES

1. *SHBL*, vol. II, p. 87.
2. *SHBL*, vol. IV, p. 315.
3. *Wuthering Heights*, ed. H. Marsden and I. Jack (Oxford, 1976) p. 437.
4. *SHBL*, vol. II, pp. 155–6.
5. *Wuthering Heights*, ed. Marsden and Jack, p. xxxiv.
6. For a clear statement about the amount of flexibility allowed to author and publisher in fitting books into one, two or three volumes, see R. Gettman, *A Victorian Publisher* (Cambridge, 1960) pp. 231–63.
7. *George Smith: A Memoir*, ed. E. Smith (London, 1902) p. 814.
8. *SHBL*, vol. III, p. 306.
9. T. Winnifrith, *The Brontës* (London, 1977) pp. 21–2.
10. Ibid., p. 20.

9 Diverging Twins: Some Clues to *Wildfell Hall*

EDWARD CHITHAM

The in-bred nature of Brontë literary influence has often been re-marked. Whereas we are quite right to see reflections of Byron, Cowper, Scott and other writers of previous generations occurring in Brontë writing, the most pervasive influence of all on each writer was the family and the other writers within it. No one has yet analysed how far Patrick Brontë's light-weight, but charming, didactic verse influenced Charlotte and Anne, for example. Branwell may not have contributed one line to *Wuthering Heights* as tradition says he did, but the parallels in plot and treatment between, say, Jabez Branderham's sermons and the Methodist meeting in *The Weary are at Rest* cannot be denied. Fraudulent publishers such as Newby made capital from the likeness of Anne's later work to *Jane Eyre*, scandalising Charlotte and Anne excessively. But in a sense Newby was right: the Brontës, while three entirely separate writers, do in a way present a combined work which to this day is sometimes presented within the same covers.[1]

Closer even than Charlotte and Emily, or Charlotte and Anne, or Charlotte and Branwell, were the two 'twins' (as Ellen Nussey called them), Emily and Anne.[2] This description of the sisters is applicable both personally and in their literary work. The personal effect of having a calmer sister, less prone to despair and incapable of being dislodged from her personal faith however sorely tried, a person of whom one might write 'How still, how happy', and who was said to have been guarded in infancy by a personal angel, was most important to Emily. She saw Anne as a co-operator, as a lighter part of herself; as one who shared the Gondal world, without whom 'merry laugh and cheerful tone' are 'fled from our fireside'.[3] But as becomes apparent in Anne's poem 'Self-Communion', as the two sisters grew up they grew away from each other; a dark river flowed between them and became impassable.

Anne, as a personality, much transmuted by Imagination, is present in many aspects of Emily's work: she contributes to Edgar and young Cathy and part of her character is seen in Gondal characters like Angelica, the rival of A. G. A., who finally aids at her death. For Emily, Anne sometimes lacked objective reality: she is allowed to draw 'a bit of Lady Julets hair' in the 1834 diary paper, but most of the paper is written by Emily. But perhaps the best use for Anne was to enable Emily to test out her thought, to have a real person present who might be relied upon to give her elder sister moral support when needed. Anne did all this, though as soon as she was out of Emily's sight, she wrote poetry of her own kind, and dropped Gondal fiction altogether.[4]

As time went on Anne's own character asserted itself. She began to see that what had previously been thought of merely as unpalatable in Emily's nature and work was actually dangerous. Witnessing the manner in which Branwell's irresponsible dreaming had been carried over into real life and had shattered his potentially comfortable life as tutor to Edmund Robinson, she began to feel compelled to resist Emily's ideas. Gondal itself was one aspect of these ideas which no longer appealed to Anne by mid-1845. She continued to play the game, but half-heartedly, as her 1845 diary paper shows.[5] Though in mid-1846 she revived her interest in it, perhaps to reconcile her sister and herself to the lack of interest on the part of publishing houses in their contributions to the three-volume novel set the 'Bells' had prepared, this phase did not last long. Next year she was working completely separate from Emily, and would never again co-operate. Ever since her experiences at Thorp Green she exhibited in all she wrote a view of life much more realistic, much more socially orientated, closer to Jane Austen or George Eliot than to Emily, or for that matter Charlotte. According to this view, 'All true histories contain instruction', though we should be very wary of taking the word 'true' at the start of *Agnes Grey* as implying literal chronological veracity. '

Anne wrote her poem 'Self-Communion' in the period between November 1847 and 17 April 1848, beginning when *Agnes Grey* and *Wuthering Heights* were on the point of publication and developing when *Wildfell Hall* was either complete or well advanced. As its title implies, it is a pensive poem, perhaps not intended for publication, which reveals the author's thoughts on various experiences of her life. Even in this poem, there is a good deal of allusion instead of outright statement, but in lines 178–207 Anne traces the development and decline of a friendship which seems to have preceded the present communion with herself.

The passage in question skips along cheerfully, beginning:

> Oh, I have known a wondrous joy
> In early friendship's pure delight, –
> A genial bliss that could not cloy –
> My sun by day, my moon by night.

That this refers to Emily can hardly be doubted, as it develops into an account of Anne's close friendship from childhood. Ellen Nussey, as has been said, records that Emily and Anne were 'like twins'. But if we have been in the habit of receiving Ellen's view unquestioned we may be in for a rough shock:

> My fondness was but half returned
> (line 187)

and

> I must check, or nurse apart
> Full many an impulse of the heart
>   And many a darling thought:
> What my soul worshipped, sought, and prized,
> Were slighted, questioned, or despised.

The words destroy at once any naïve notion of total harmony between the sisters. Anne continues with a metaphor of the two friends bending over the brink of a dark stream, by which they are as much divided as linked. She continues:

> Until at last, I learned to bear
> A colder heart within my breast;
> To share such thoughts as I could share,
>   And calmly keep the rest.

This would seem to indicate Emily's disdain for ideas which she found unsympathetic. The passage ends with a further metaphor, this time of two trees which 'at the root were one', but of which the stems must stand alone though they might still touch leaves and boughs. The image is an effective one, occurring in the other sisters' work too. It ought to dispose of the idea that Anne is a dull poet. For our present purpose it serves as an illumination of the attitudes of the two sisters towards each other at the period after the publication of *Wuthering Heights* and before that of *Wildfell Hall*. Anne sees herself divided from her sister by a 'dark stream'; as one of a pair of trees rooted together, but now 'sundered'.

One might of course object that Emily is not named. While this is true, it is impossible to produce any other candidate for the role of jointly-rooted tree. Charlotte might possibly be considered, but we have Ellen Nussey's testimony, even if there were not many other pieces of external evidence, to show that it was Emily and Anne who were considered 'twins'; and in any case there is the whole lengthy collaboration in Gondal to support the notion. We must conclude that it is Emily to whom Anne has been close, and that in the winter of 1847–8, she regarded their former communion as over.

With this in mind, we might look carefully at Anne's poem 'The Three Guides' of 11 August 1847. It was Muriel Spark who first pointed out that the 'Spirit of Pride' who appears at stanza 10 might well be the spirit currently guiding Emily, and that Anne might be offering a criticism of Emily's attitudes here. As she says in *Emily Brontë*, 'one cannot avoid the conclusion that Anne was guying Emily in more ways than one'.[6]

Anne's 'three guides' are the spirits of 'earth', 'Pride' and 'Faith'. She concludes by accepting the hand of Faith as she goes on her journey since,

> By thy help, all things I can do;
> In thy strength all things bear,

but not before she has argued forcefully against the other two guides. The possibility that the poem adopts its trinity from Emily's 'The Philosopher', with its warring gods, must be borne in mind. There has also been a suggestion that the three guides may represent the three characters and inclinations of Charlotte, Emily and Anne respectively. It is hard to see Charlotte as a 'spirit of earth', but the idea is not impossible. However, what is clearer is that the attitudes exhibited by 'Spirit of Pride' do reflect those of the major characters in *Wuthering Heights*, especially Heathcliff and Catherine.

The moral purport of the novel has worried critics, beginning with Charlotte, whose well-known reservation ('Whether it is right or desirable to create beings like Heathcliff I do not know') may echo private family comment made during the book's formation.[7] In Anne's poem Pride is said to have strong wings and eyes like lightning, just as Heathcliff's are those of a basilisk. The eyes of Pride are 'fascinating', but it is a 'false destructive blaze'. Pride replies to this accusation by telling the poet to 'pasture with thy fellow sheep', intending a sneer, though Anne seems to be exploiting the Christian associations of the word, as though suggesting to Emily that the 'Spirit' she longs to see in 'The Philosopher' is to be identified with the Good Shepherd of Christianity. Heathcliff's remark that 'the more the worms writhe the more I long to stamp out their entrails' may be echoed in stanza 12 with its 'Cling to the earth, poor grovelling worm!', while Emily's description of the released soul in 'Julian M. and A. G. Rochelle' (H190), lines 83–4, 'Its wings are almost free, its home, its harbour found / Measuring the gulf it stoops and dares the final bound' may be referred to in Anne's description of the proud soul which 'Sustained a while by thee / O'er rocks of ice and hills of snow / Bound fearless, wild and free'.

The fact is that even as far back as the poems of late 1837 there is a difference of emphasis: Anne's happily reunited lovers in 'Alexander and Zenobia' do not find a counterpart in Emily's work. Anne's characters in this poem are joyful, trusting, sympathetic and genuinely attached, while Emily's already seem to exhibit excessive emotions and at times to talk in Byronic clichés. Anne was in fact showing indifference to Gondal from the beginning of the 1840s, and from then on only seems to have played at Gondal in order to humour Emily. Meanwhile, she had her own concerns which Emily did not share: an absorbed commitment to the 'Narrow Way' of evangelical Christianity, and a passion for education. Emily meanwhile had rejected orthodoxy and was endlessly concerned to reconcile the warring elements within her: violence and tenderness, pride and humility. Both girls wrote poems in which they used birds as self-symbols: Anne's is 'The Captive Dove', Emily's a bird of the hills with shining eyes and the characteristics of a falcon.[8]

At the age of six, Emily set out to join her three elder sisters at Cowan Bridge School. Since in the poems she several times mentions six as a time for crucial experience we may be led to suppose that this age had subconsciously made a mark on her. Mrs Chadwick quotes the Clergy School registers on Emily's report as follows:

Entered Nov. 25, 1824, age 5¾. Reads very prettily, and works a little. Left June 1, 1825. Subsequent career, governess.[9]

The superintendent, Miss Evans, said she was 'quite the pet nursling of the school'.[10] She was one of the younger children at the time she entered, though there were very small girls there and one cannot rely too heavily on Miss Evans' memory.[11] Any deductions about Emily's feelings at Cowan Bridge must be speculative, but her subsequent ventures into school life were notably less than happy. There is no recorded case of Emily being contented in a crowd or allowing any of her characters in novel or poetry to be so. We may wonder therefore if the pet nursling was sometimes sulky or bit the hand that fed it. The several poems in which small children feel alienated and sulky in crowds suggest that Cowan Bridge was as unpropitious for tiny Emily as for Charlotte. By the time she was brought back from school, staying one night at Silverdale, her mother-substitute, Maria, was dead. One hesitates therefore to agree with Winifred Gerin, who in writing of Branwell's mourning for Maria says, 'The early deaths of her sisters had no comparable effect on Emily. Nor do the teaching or the sufferings of Cowan Bridge appear to have left any mark on her.'[12] After Cowan Bridge, Emily hated schools. After Maria's death, Emily was perpetually haunted by presences from another world; the archetype of the resentful orphan was often in her mind. Anne did not hate schools and at Miss Wooler's she won a prize. She took on herself the moral education of the Robinson girls long after she had left the paid service of the household. Unlike Emily she was at home when Maria died there, and was able to repeat her calm death when her own turn came at Scarborough in 1849. Thus the early life experience of the two 'twins' differs considerably, with Anne not unsocialised by precipitate experience of school discipline and her feelings concerning the ultimate destination of 'good' human souls not flouted and made uncertain by the sudden removal and disappearance of her loved elder sister.

There followed an intense period of imaginative and literary activity. The four remaining Brontës paired off and the juvenilia we have is all in the handwriting of the elder pair. References are made to the younger girls, but nothing they wrote has so far been identified. Out of the shared dramas Gondal was formed, though no one knows when. We find the earliest reference to it in the 1834 diary paper. The date of this paper is precisely ten years to the day from the night when the 'pet nursling' was being got ready for her journey to Cowan Bridge. As for 'Lady Julet', whose hair Anne drew, she disappears and is never heard of again. Ellen's twins were working together: but one twin was more equal than the other.

It is probably no accident that the earliest preserved poems of Emily and Anne date from 1836. Earlier ones may have been destroyed in a parental holocaust.[13] All the work from 1836 by both sisters is Gondal-based, and this continues to be true of all unequivocally dated material up to the middle of 1837. Emily was discovering in herself an insistent drive towards poetic expression which was to make itself clearly felt in the next two years while Anne produced work of charm but no depth on Gondal topics.

But after arriving at Thorp Green Anne began to write poetry increasingly divergent from Emily's and quite independent in tone. Gondal content is rare throughout the years with the Robinsons, and a strongly introspective and religious element enters. Anne is reading Cowper with attention and during the next years begins her collection of hymns and religious poems, a genre which was apparently anathema to Emily.[14] Separation becomes a common theme, but is very different-ly treated by the two sisters. Anne concentrates on moral separation, either from God or from fellow humans, and this theme steadily becomes one of the mainstays of her work.

By the time she wrote *Wildfell Hall*, as we shall see, Anne was intensely occupied with the problem of separation from the loved one who has sinned. That such people might be condemned to eternal punishment was impossible to Anne's thought, and she was driven by her logic to explore further the material of 'A word to the Calvinists'. Confronted with similar problems, Emily makes no attempt to recon-cile the opposites: her poems partake much more of emotional expres-sion of the contradictions, rather than attempts to reconcile or har-monise them. Her main fear appears to have been separation from the loved one in a physical sense, and it was intuition and visionary light, rather than logic, which ruled her mind.

The year 1846 is a critical one for the literary development of Emily and Anne Brontë. Emily had at first been most reluctant to publish her poetry, but in the end had succumbed to Charlotte's persuasion; Anne had proved more pliant. Both sisters were to see themselves in print by May 1846; but the knowledge that they had stepped on to a public stage affected them very differently. It is hard to see Anne's poem 'Domestic Peace' (Charlotte's 1850 title) as a poem merely about Branwell's restlessness and decline:

> Each feels the bliss of all destroyed
> And mourns the change – but each apart.
>
> We rudely drove thee from our hearth
> And vainly sigh for thy return.

The final couplet was radically altered by Charlotte when she came to print the poem. It seems reasonable to assume that there was general dissension at this time, partly no doubt as a result of Branwell's despair, but also because Emily and Anne were on divergent paths.

Hardly had the poems appeared than the first three Brontë novels began their rounds of publishing houses.[15] That *Agnes Grey* was being written during 1845 seems certain, whether or not it developed from 'Passages in the Life of an Individual' mentioned in Anne's 1845 diary paper. Knowing Emily's methods of writing, we may suspect that the snowy opening chapters of *Wuthering Heights* were formed as early as February or March 1845; February was the coldest since 1838 and March the coldest since 1807. There were heavy snowfalls about the middle of the month and temperatures throughout the previous six weeks had been very much below average.[16] 'Cold in the Earth', an exceptionally fine Gondal poem, is dated 3 March 1845; its tenor and content are much akin to *Wuthering Heights*, Chapter 3. The winter of 1845–6 was milder and no heavy falls of snow are recorded. It would be rash to press too hard the observation that Emily Brontë wrote of weather she was actually experiencing at the time, but the thick snow of early 1845 may provide at least a clue to the date of composition of the early parts of the novel. The next occasion on which very heavy snow fell was November/December 1846.

During August 1846 Charlotte went with her father to Manchester for his eye operation. On 26 August, she received *The Professor* back from the latest publisher.[17] We may assume that Emily and Anne had sent it on from Haworth after extracting their own novels from the rejected parcel. There is not a word of external evidence on how they felt about their rebuff, but on 14 September they both worked on new Gondal poems, suggesting that they may have decided to retreat for the moment from attempts to publish fiction, perhaps to publish at all. Anne's poem shows a development from her earlier work, evidence of increasing self-confidence. Emily's was a long, unsatisfactory, much altered and never finished narrative: it turned out to be the last poem she ever wrote, and she was still revising it in 1848. Next month Anne wrote her last Gondal poem. Though she had two-and-a-half years to live and would write important poetry, there was no more of Gondal. Knowing that she had hardly ever written Gondal poems on her own account but always almost in conjunction with Emily, one might well suppose that she had decided that constant regression to this childhood game was detrimental to her sister and might harm herself. While there is no external evidence of dissension between the sisters between 1846 and Emily's death, and they must have co-operated at least so far as to send off *Agnes Grey* and the perhaps revised *Wuthering Heights* to Newby, yet we have Anne's statement, earlier referred to, that she had to learn to keep her thoughts to herself.

That there is a strong similarity between some of the external characteristics of *Wildfell Hall* and *Wuthering Heights* is of course a commonplace. For that matter *Jane Eyre* too has its links with these two. In part these similarities stem from common Brontë preoccupations. But we must also bear in mind that *Wuthering Heights* was apparently written in 1845–6, while *Wildfell Hall* looks as though it was produced in 1847, though it may have been started before this. Gilbert Markham's 'closing' date, 'June 10th 1847' may indeed be a starting date or an intermediate date: but it is hard to suppose that it means nothing at all. We need also to take into account the great *differences* between *Wuthering Heights* and *Wildfell Hall*, which, bearing in mind the similarities of title, setting up similar expectations, seem unlikely to be accidental. Very important also is Anne's preface to the second printing, dated 22 July 1848.[18] A study of this makes quite clear Anne's motives in novel writing, which are clearly somewhat different from those of Emily.

'I wished to tell the truth, for truth always conveys its own moral to those who are able to receive it', is the first key sentence; 'and if I can gain the public ear at all, I would rather whisper a few wholesome truths therein than much soft nonsense'. Anne, then, will put truth first, and will have no truck with these novelists who like to write 'soft nonsense' (in this phrase the word 'soft' is clearly intended colloquially, and does not imply 'weak' but 'silly'). She goes on to defend herself against charges of coarseness and brutality, saying, 'when we have to do with Vice and vicious characters, I maintain it is better to depict them as they really are than as they would wish to appear', and she admits that she found the writing of such scenes painful. Charlotte supports this in the 'Memoir':

She hated her work, but would pursue it. When reasoned with on the subject, she regarded such reasonings as a temptation to self-indulgence. She must be honest: she must not varnish, soften or conceal.

Is it possible that Anne, reading or listening to *Wuthering Heights*, might consider her sister had in a way 'varnished' or 'concealed' the truth, and that in writing *Wildfell Hall* she intended in part to correct her sister's view? It seems possible at any rate that the resemblances between the two novels are deliberate, and that the differences are intended to highlight what Anne may have thought of as the inadequacies of her sister's philosophical outlook, which she saw expressed in the novel. Let us begin with the resemblances, starting with the obvious externals of title and nomenclature. 'Wuthering' is, as we are told, a 'significant provincial adjective'. Anne uses no provincial adjective in her title, but she does use words that echo Emily's, and in particular names that begin with the same initial letters. It is curious that a group of Emily's characters have names beginning with H: Hindley, Hareton, Heathcliff. The resulting confusion, paralleled by her use of names in the Gondal poems, is surely alluded to by Anne when she chooses the names Huntingdon, Hargrave, Halford, Hattersley and Helen. It is playful satire, perhaps, but it surely is satire of a kind. We have seen Anne as satirist in *Agnes Grey*, so this approach need not surprise us. Lockwood is a fop; Anne struggles to make her hero a foppish young man, whose character develops and so eventually gains our sympathy. (That she is not quite successful here does not necessarily invalidate my point.)[19] In both stories the starting point is the arrival of a new tenant in a remote house in the North; but in Anne's novel the romantic possibilities of such an event are discarded as 'varnish', and we are made to see the practical rigours and difficulties of life in a decaying mansion. Wuthering Heights is a house approved of by its author for its mystery, its ghosts, and its warm fires: Wildfell Hall is an unromantic shell for most of the novel, and its 'ghostly legends and dark traditions' are not even told, let alone exploited.[20]

The other themes which the novels share include marital unfaithfulness, drunkenness, violence and the question of life after death. On all these topics the sisters occupy very different positions, and it is hard not to see Anne's novel as a corrective to Emily's 'soft nonsense'.

Seen from this angle *Wuthering Heights* is 'about' a young girl who marries hastily and who reverts to a former allegiance, scorning her husband and humiliating him. Anne might perhaps have argued that while Edgar Linton is at times quite kindly portrayed, we are never allowed to see things from his point of view. In *Wildfell Hall* we are allowed to see much of the story of the originally pacific Helen, the wronged party in marriage, through her own eyes. In part, Anne's aim is to show us adultery from the less romantic aspect. (That this is not *all* her intention I would strongly maintain, as can be seen by my note in *The Poems of Anne Brontë* on poem 55, p. 193.) Anne is not convinced by Emily's portrayal of the 'demon lover' theme; she appears to suspect that in real life the power of a demon to hurt will wear away love. In treating this story of adultery, Anne displays considerable powers of characterisation. Lady Lowborough, for example, though much disapproved of, is in some ways an attractive character whose appeal to Huntingdon we can well understand. Anne is not interested in stereotypes, and the evidence of her careful observation and skilled delineation suggests that she would have continued to write good novels if she had lived. Certainly one feels the force of 'I wished to tell the truth' in such a character as Lady Lowborough.

There is, too, a great contrast in the approach of the two writers to violence. As an example, we may take the account of the brutal attack Heathcliff makes on Hindley Earnshaw in Chapter 17 of *Wuthering Heights*. Heathcliff flings himself against Hindley, who has a gun and loaded pistol. The gun goes off, and the knife 'closed into the owner's wrist. Heathcliff pulled it away by main force, slitting up the flesh as it passed on, and thrust it dripping into his pocket'. The colour of the knife at this point is not mentioned, and when two sentences later Hindley falls 'senseless with excessive pain' we do not feel the pain at all. The mere fact is recorded, and is ascribed to the loss of blood from 'an artery, or a large vein'. Heathcliff then lifts up his victim and dashes his head 'repeatedly' against the flags. Hindley does not die, though next morning he is sitting by the fire, 'deadly sick'. The story is put into the mouth of Isabella, and in the excitement we do not notice its improbability, or how Emily has allowed us to avoid the feeling of cruelty on the one side or sickening pain on the other. After roughly binding up his victim (one wonders why), Heathcliff tells Joseph to 'Wash that stuff away' (referring to the blood which we may imagine to be soaking the stone floor), and then pushes him 'in the middle of the blood'.

The description of the brawl and Heathcliff's murderous outburst is as schematic as it could possibly be. No adjective is used of the blood pouring down Hindley's face and body, we do not see or feel the bruises surely resulting from the repeated thumping of his inanimate head on the floor, and in fact the assertion that Hindley is still alive next morning is frankly unbelievable unless Isabella has been allowed to exaggerate his injuries. Emily has quite deliberately glossed over the terrible squalor and pain of the scene and has evaded bringing home to the reader how destructive such violence could be. Such episodes only show, of course, that Emily is not interested in the production of realistic novels, but one might well expect Anne to be unsympathetic to this approach.

In the preface to the second printing of *Wildfell Hall* she is quick to defend herself from the charge of loving 'the brutal', and says that 'those scenes . . . have not been more painful for the most fastidious of my critics to read than they were for me to describe'. One such scene may be her answer to the one just quoted from *Wuthering Heights*. Critics have sometimes been puzzled to know why it is that Gilbert Markham, the rather effeminate hero of *Wildfell Hall* is described furiously attacking his friend Lawrence at the beginning of Chapter 14. The motive of jealousy is urged by the author, but she does not seem to be quite successful in making us believe the violence this provokes. The explanation may perhaps be that Anne has here allowed her moral sense to mar her sense of character. The assault on Lawrence is not required by the plot, and not required by what we know of Gilbert Markham: but it is required if Anne is concerned to show in her novel the dangers of portraying violence in such a balladic way as in *Wuthering Heights*. She has to find a place in her book to introduce a scene of violence, and she either makes a wrong choice, or else fails sufficiently to prepare the reader for the episode.

The attack begins with an exchange between the two which is notable on Lawrence's side for its courtesy. But Markham, 'impelled by some fiend at my elbow', lifts his whip and savagely brings the butt down upon Lawrence's head – once. With a feeling of savage satisfaction he sees the 'instant deadly pallor' overspread his face, and watches the 'few red drops' trickle down his forehead. Not for Markham repeated banging on the floor of his victim's head while a 'large vein' pours forth blood. Very soon he thinks 'Had I killed him?', and decides he cannot summon any friendly feeling for Lawrence, unlike Heath-cliff who tore up Hindley's shirt for bandages. Returning later he finds Lawrence 'Looking very white and sickly still' with dirty clothes and a reddened handkerchief held to his head.

Surely this is Anne's attempt to delineate a violent attack and its consequences in a realistic way? The stark excesses of Emily's scene are avoided as unbelievable, and feeling re-enters. We are forced to watch Lawrence's face grow pale, and to share Markham's guilt as he tries to excuse himself for the attack, 'It served him right – it would teach him better manners in future.' Detail is stressed: 'the few red drops', 'his clothes considerably bemired', the handkerchief 'now saturated with blood', and 'He had risen from the ground, and grasping his pony's mane, was attempting to resume his seat in the saddle; but scarcely had he put his foot in the stirrup, when a sickness or dizziness seemed to overpower him.' In reading this, we can understand the sense of both Charlotte's words and Anne's own: she has forced herself to imagine and describe this scene simply because 'truth always conveys its own moral to those who are able to receive it'; truth of this kind, by implication, is not to be found in *Wuthering Heights*.

It is interesting that all the Brontës write intensely about marital infidelity. The biographical background in the case of Branwell and Charlotte is well known, but of course this real life encounter with the problem had been preceded by endless youthful exploration of the theme in the Angrian saga, which treats notional adultery as a matter of course, though it does not explore the feeling of the parties with much psychological insight. The young Brontës seem to have thought of the excitement of jealousy and revenge as dominant emotions, their apparent sources being historical romance, ballads and perhaps particularly the works of Byron. When Charlotte and Branwell each found the topic, in different ways, entering their own lives, the subject became one of frustrated love rather than careless faithlessness.

Emily's treatment of adultery in Gondal seems to be the most schematic, and the emotions caused by it have no ring of truth. The characters involved plainly have no counterparts in life. Edgar, Heathcliff and Catherine, on the other hand, do have a very stark and intense life, and the validity of their emotions, even Edgar's less violent ones, is not in doubt. Many critics have seen them as mythic or balladic figures, living very much in the spirit and little in the body. Despite the earlier view that Branwell was in some way portrayed in Heathcliff, Emily avoids any parallel with Branwell's personal story and no character in *Wuthering Heights* remotely resembles the bored, excitable, worldly yet religious woman whom we meet in most accounts of Mrs Lydia Robinson. The *dramatis personae* of *Wuthering Heights* are not drawn from life, unless from the very vivid internal life of their creator.

But this is not true of the characters in *Wildfell Hall*. All of them are flawed, and in many ways, though none are villains. Huntingdon, Anne's anti-hero, is just the kind of man to sweep an impressionable girl off her feet, with his 'Sweet angel, I adore you!', but Helen admits that he is not a man of principle: 'it is only for want of thought.... I should think my life well spent in the effort to preserve so noble a nature from destruction.' In this scene Anne captures beautifully the reforming zeal of Romantic girlhood, so dear to the writers of Victorian fiction. She then shows through the book that it will not work. Helen, though truly a heroine, is no flawless saint.

So when infidelity is contemplated, Arthur Huntingdon succumbs, while Helen herself survives the specious advances of Hargrave, only to find herself genuinely tempted by the more honest though insensitive admiration of Markham. Here we see no bold defiance of custom, or attempt to have one's cake and eat it, as in the case of Catherine, but a careful exploration of the conflicts arising in Helen, first from being the victim of infidelity, then of being sorely tempted to succumb herself not to a demonic Heathcliff, nor even a Romantic Rochester, but to a yeoman farmer with few pretensions to gentility, even though he does read *Marmion*. In the handling of this theme we see an author with totally different aims, interested in character and emotional conflict in the live world, without any reference to the poetic and transcendental world of Emily's dream. It is hard not to see this contrast as part of Anne's rejection of her sister's 'soft nonsense'.

Anne does more than explore character. She engages very seriously with the main theme of Brontë adolescent writing and conscientiously explores its causes and context. Infidelity, it seems, results from inadequate education, especially of the male. Young Arthur is tightly controlled, though this brings rebuke from the conventional Mrs Markham. Through Helen, Anne refutes the notion that girls need to be closely guarded while boys range free; in fact, 'if I thought he would grow up to be what you call a man of the world . . . I would rather that he died tomorrow'. Boys need as much care as girls, though conventional wisdom regards girls as the more tender plants. It is thus not the case that Emily's views are unconventional, while Anne's are conventional, but that there is no parallel between the sisters in their unconventionality.

That Edgar, Cathy and Heathcliff sleep together in their graves does not necessarily appear to have been an idea offensive to Anne, for she boldly tackles this view of their future in a discussion of the kind of love which may subsist in heaven. The ardent Markham is enjoined not to contact Helen for six months, protests, and is told that he will meet her again in heaven. The fact that he may meet her as a disembodied spirit gives him 'little consolation'; she reassures him, but he finds it hard to look forward to a state in which she 'will have no closer sympathy with me than any one of the ten thousand thousand angels . . . round us'. Helen replies in faith that 'we know it must be for the better', and Markham counters with 'my earthly nature cannot rejoice in the anticipation of such beatitude'. When Helen asks 'Is your love all earthly?' he reverts to the fear that he will lose precedence with her and will be no more attached than the other spirits. This is in direct contrast to the future union proposed by Cathy and Heathcliff, for all that it includes Edgar. Anne insists that future love between humans will be ideal, and all-inclusive, and allows Helen an almost platonic passage to expand this idea. Thus she wishes to solve the problem of jealousy, not by envisaging a future state when lovers will be mutually attached for ever, even though this love has to be extended to include a third party, but by contemplating a heaven in which the intensity of love felt for individuals on earth will be strengthened so as to include all other persons and jealousy will disappear. That this idea results from the resolution of her conflicts, and that it is a hard won conviction, is suggested by the series of poems concerned with Anne's relations with William Weightman, and in particular by the final stanza of her poem no. 55, 'Severed and Gone'.

It is perfectly clear that Emily Brontë cannot conceive of a universe in which there is no relation between the dead and the living. Her poems and novel take two views on the matter, which are intertwined and do not seem to be regarded as mutually contradictory. The first view is that man's personal identity is lost at death:

> Oh, for a time when I shall sleep
> Without identity.

But this Housman-like view of death (perhaps in his case too influenced by Horace, Housman's idol, and well translated by Branwell) does not prevent Emily from the continual encounter with disembodied spirits: nor is it quite fair to suggest that in this view death is an end, since the metaphor of sleep is so often used in this context, and a sleeper, though unconscious, does not cease totally to exist.

Emily's other view, exemplified in such poems as 'Aye there it is!' sees death as a release from the prison of the body. On this view the 'dungeon' which has entombed the spirit during its life will turn to mould at death, leaving the soul to return to heaven:

> Thus truly when that breast is cold
> Thy prisoned soul shall rise,
> The dungeon mingle with the mould –
> The captive with the skies.

This poem, like others, is wholly Pantheist in tone, closest to Shelley, but echoing the long tradition of Pythagoras and Plato in a manner that is certainly Pagan, without any Christian nuance.

Anne's understanding of death on the other hand is expressed entirely in Christian terms even when she is on the verge of heresy.

One of her aims in *Wildfell Hall* is to explore the problem of hell after death (Emily at times suggests hell is on earth), and in particular the notion of hell as a force which separates and will separate. Thus in Chapter 47, when Arthur Huntingdon is in a delirium which has points of contact with that of Cathy in *Wuthering Heights*, he raises the moral problem of how souls in heaven can be happy knowing that others, including perhaps those they have loved, will be in hell. Typical of his understanding is the remark that Helen's care for him is 'an act of Christian charity, whereby you hope to gain a higher seat in heaven for yourself, and scoop a deeper pit in hell for me'. Of this kind of pleasure, Anne had already written, 'May God withhold such cruel joy from me!' Throughout the scene, the railing of Arthur at his wife bears similarities to that of Cathy against Heathcliff, but the total failure of understanding between the pair in *Wildfell Hall* produces a second level of pathos as we see the matter from Arthur's viewpoint, in a way which is totally absent from the intenser novel. In these deathbed scenes Anne goes some way towards a successful portrayal of the heavily limited Arthur, and secures our pity for him not only for his physical strait, but for his very lack of generosity, which will not accept his wife's residual love. There is no parallel in *Wuthering Heights*, which has entirely different aims.

Two chapters later Anne returns to the problem of heaven and hell as Arthur reaches his end. Here we have a most telling contrast with that of Heathcliff, who thinks in terms of unity with Cathy and for whom, as he starves himself to death 'My heaven is almost in sight'. Helen assures Arthur that when he is 'howling in hell-fire' (as he puts it), she will rest herself only if she is assured that he is 'being purified from your sins, and fitted to enjoy the happiness I felt'. Heathcliff's heaven is union with Cathy: Helen's is union with God and (as Anne's Universalism verges on heresy in nineteenth-century eyes) with all creatures, duly purified to take their place there.

Anne, it must be remembered, is writing of the death of Huntingdon *in the light of the death of Heathcliff*. She wishes to show us the death of a man who has been wicked on earth and is still far separated from help. He is certainly not in sight of his heaven; even on Anne's generous interpretation of the New Testament passages Helen has studied, he will need lengthy purification before being fit to live with God. As Anne puts it in her preface, 'when I feel it my duty to speak an unpalatable truth, with the help of God, I *will* speak it, though it be to the prejudice of my name and to the detriment of my reader's immediate pleasure as well as my own'. She will therefore contradict

Emily's easy view of the attainment of heaven, just as she will contradict the view of the orthodox that hell is eternal.

'One more word, and I have done', she finishes. 'I would have it distinctly understood that Acton Bell is neither Currer nor Ellis Bell.' This strong disclaimer is regarded as natural by literary historians, who attribute it to Anne's honesty (she adds, 'let not his faults be attributed to them'). But in asserting her independence she is also pointing out the need to judge her work, with its message, on its own terms, not to confuse Heathcliff and Huntingdon, Markham and Lockwood. Yet this is still too often done, and Anne's book is seen as a weak addendum to *Wuthering Heights* rather than a staunch criticism of it.

There are other aspects of *Wildfell Hall* which correct *Wuthering Heights*. Drink makes Hindley titanic in his rage; but it makes Hattersley and the rest stupid. They brawl inconsequentially and tip tea into the sugar basin. When Arthur himself is drunk he is feebly nasty, as Branwell appears to have become petty and incapable of firm action when he had been too often to the Black Bull. Anne clearly sees alcoholism as a personal and social evil, and allows Helen space to give a detailed description of her method of training a child to reject drink. It is of course very easy to object that a novel is not intended to be the place for such a didactic approach. Anne, however, is in a tradition as old at least as Swift, and her work also partakes of the serious purpose of *Pilgrim's Progress*, that now neglected book so close to evangelical hearts in the early nineteenth century.

Lockwood dreams of a sermon and becomes bored with his dream. The dream satire is superbly effective, but viewed from the angle of a writer conscientiously fishing for men, Emily's satire does nothing to reconcile us to the truth of the points made by the irritating Branderham. Arthur Huntingdon also listens to a sermon, during which he makes a caricature of the preacher, giving him the air 'of a most absurd old hypocrite'. His conduct during the service is disliked by Helen, but she is not warned, as she should be, by this and other pointers to his true character.

Heathcliff is apparently discovered in the slums of Liverpool, and though Nelly speculates that his father might be 'Emperor of China, and your mother an Indian Queen', he is soon degraded and belittled. Despite Nelly's romantic view of his possible ancestry he is more often thought of as a gypsy, a little lascar, and, as some writers have thought, illegitimate. There are signs, though, that Emily considers his birth and upbringing justify his penetrating revenge, and a school of critics would almost see him as a heroic representative of the underdog, the

Victorian working-class exacting its due from the landowning squires.

Anne shows that she agrees that one's family and upbringing have to be taken into account in prophesying one's future. Helen wishes to give Huntingdon the chance to shake off 'the adventitious evil got from contact with others worse than himself, and shining out in the un- clouded light of his own genuine goodness', and in so saying speaks much like a starry-eyed follower of Rousseau, or a reader of Wordsworth's 'Immortality' ode. In her ardour she is far from remem- bering the Christian notion of original sin, and puts down Arthur's worse characteristics to his 'bad, selfish, miserly father' who 'disgusted him with every kind of restraint'. One main theme of the book is her failure to reform him, though even at this point she refuses a simplistic account of human nature which would equate her with light, Arthur with darkness: 'I am not light, and he is not darkness; his worst and only vice is thoughtlessness.'[21]

Such 'thoughtlessness' besets most of the characters of *Wuthering Heights* most of the time. They are agents of higher powers within themselves, seen by critics as 'storm' or 'calm'. Anne is determined to show human nature 'as it really is', far removed from the mythic world of the heights. Like her sister's novel, *Wildfell Hall* is concerned with love, marriage, death and the supernatural, drink and violence, heaven and hell; it is organised in a manner parodying *Wuthering Heights* (Emily and Anne even used the same almanacs from the 1820s to construct their elaborate and accurate timescales).[22] This parallelism cannot be accidental, but must surely be part of Anne's final answer to her sister in some degree intended to balance the 'wild' characters at the heights and thus make use of the novel for what Anne saw to be its aim, 'to reform the errors and abuses of society'.

NOTES

1. For example in the popular Spring Books edition.
2. E. Nussey, 'Reminiscences of Charlotte Brontë', *Scribner's Monthly*, vol. II (May 1871) p. 26.
3. H97.
4. See E. Chitham, *The Poems of Anne Brontë* (London, 1979) Introduc- tion.
5. Transcript in C. K. Shorter, *Charlotte Brontë and her Circle* (London, 1896) pp. 152–3.
6. M. Spark and D. Stanford, *Emily Brontë* (London, 1959) p. 89.
7. E. Gaskell, *The Life of Charlotte Brontë* (London, 1857) Chapter 15,

tells of the sisters' habit of reading over their work to each other while in the process of composition.

8. Compare E. Chitham, *The Poems of Anne Brontë*, p. 92 and H144.
9. Quoted by W. Gerin, *Emily Brontë* (Oxford, 1971) p. 8.
10. Ibid.
11. For the ages of children on admission, see Dobson, *Notes on the Clergy Daughters' School, Casterton* (Beverley, 1935) Paper II.
12. Gerin, *Emily Brontë*, p. 9.
13. For substantiation of this suggestion, see Chitham, *The Poems of Anne Brontë*, p. 27.
14. See Chapter 6.
15. W. Gerin, *Charlotte Brontë* (Oxford, 1967) pp. 310–11.
16. *London, Edinburgh and Dublin Philosophical Magazine*, vol. XXVI (January–June 1845).
17. Gerin, *Charlotte Brontë*, p. 327.
18. Printed, for example, in G. D. Hargreaves' edition of *The Tenant of Wildfell Hall* (Harmondsworth, 1979).
19. See, for example, Kingsley's review, *Fraser's Magazine* (April 1849).
20. *Wildfell Hall*, Chapter 2.
21. Cf. also Chapters 30 and 31, in which Helen struggles to avoid the taint of complicity in Arthur's 'degradation'.
22. See Appendix to the Clarendon edition of *Wuthering Heights*, ed. H. Marsden and I. Jack (Oxford, 1976).

10 The Development of 'Vision' in Emily Brontë's Poems

EDWARD CHITHAM

Emily Brontë has often been described as a 'mystic' and many critics have touched on this aspect of her poetry.[1] As we have seen, one aspect of this visionary approach may have been derived from the Romantics. In this essay I shall examine some of the poems in which spirits or nocturnal visions are featured, taking into account some passages in late poems, a major function of which seems to be to explore such visionary and imaginary gifts. This exploration will supplement that of the previous chapter.

It is of course begging the question to assume that such visions can fairly be described as imaginary, or imaginative. The one adjective throws doubt on the objective reality Emily describes, the other patronisingly seems to suggest some kind of wilful or capricious faculty such as that which Mr Gradgrind thinks he is attacking in *Hard Times*. That Emily sometimes imagined on purpose is clear from some of her Gondal work, and I have suggested elsewhere that she consciously used this kind of deliberate fantasising to pad out poetic material which she could not otherwise complete.[2] This fictional invention is often at a low artistic and spiritual level; a good example is presented by the unevenness of 'Silent is the House', where there may exist a case for dismembering the poem. This is certainly not the only case in Emily Brontë's work of surface material being used to patch up genuine poetry. I should maintain that Gondal poetry is often an amalgam of stanzas and groups of lines which reflect Emily's deeper interests and a host of inconsequential Gondal ephemera which is simply not worth reading as poetry, though it may have biographical interest. Despite this, and though avowedly non-Gondal material naturally provides the

110

best guide to the nature of Emily's experiences, Gondal characters may sometimes act or talk in ways which can be paralleled by a record of what we know of Emily's own elusive mind, and thus show their identity with their creator. It must be remembered, however, that the dangers of circular argument are great.

Some poems which we can accurately date early show a vivid concern with nightmare. The two best examples are those occurring on MSS D2 and D4 (H12 and H15).[3] These date from 10 June 1837 and 7 August 1837 respectively. The first two stanzas of no. 12 tell of waking up from a night of storm. It is likely that the night was in fact stormy; Shackleton records thunder on that date, and considerable rain fell.[4] In lines 7 and 8 the poet speaks of troubling 'visions', and goes on to record a dream, which may or may not correspond with the poet's actual experience. The next stanza introduces 'royal corpses' on a marble tomb. These are clearly Gondal in form, and their stylisation leaves room for doubt about their reality. But royalty was at the forefront of English minds at the time, with Queen Victoria at the beginning of her reign.

The next stanzas describe the presence of a 'shadowy thing' which the poet mortally fears. The effect of the vision was to induce paralysis; the dreamer's prayers are null and limbs immobile. The last verse carries conviction:

> O bring not back again
> The horror of that hour
> When its lips opened, and a sound
> Awoke the reigning stillness round,
> Faint as a dream, but the earth shrank
> And heaven's lights shivered 'neath its power.[5]

It should be noticed that this description carefully avoids Gothic trappings, and that the culmination of the vision's paralysing effect is the emission of an unearthly sound. This unearthly sound, sometimes described as a positive, sometimes a negative experience, enters several other poems of Emily Brontë. One might remember in this context that sharp-eyed as Emily was, she was especially noted for her musical performances on the piano and was undoubtedly receptive to all kinds of sound, such as the dry scratching sound of fir cones on a window, which she uses in *Wuthering Heights*, Chapter III, just before Lockwood awakes from his dreams with a yell, a yell which he finds on waking was not merely 'ideal'. In this famous passage, just as in the poem we are discussing, sound plays a central part.

In a popular work on dreams and nightmares, *The Dream Game*, Ann Faraday says:

> The incubus attack includes the night terror ... of children (and some adults) which often culminates in a blood-curdling scream, palpitations, choking and a feeling of paralysis.[6]

The description is close enough to Emily's poem to make it seem likely that she had experienced this kind of nightmare and was possibly suffering from it at the period in question. The cause of such an attack is uncertain, but it often occurs early in the night, is fairly frequent among children, and may reflect some kind of psychic conflict.

Many poems of Emily Brontë describe the subject awake late at night, as for example H114, where Emily is in a pleasantly drowsy state at midnight, but not proposing to go to bed, and H46, in which 'Ierne' ('The Irish one') hears the clock strike one. One can of course deny the identification of poet with creation in these two cases as in almost every other specified case. But there is external biographical evidence to suggest that Emily went to sleep late, perhaps to avoid attacks of nightmare like those mentioned in poem H12.

Turning to the next nightmare poem, H15, we find the poet expressing thanks that 'the dream of horror / The frightful dream is over now'.[7] The description of the dream is much vaguer this time, and appears to allegorise and use vocabulary drawn from Gothic exemplars. Among the symptoms are burning tears, groans, staring eyes, impatient rage and more interestingly 'a soul that was for ever thinking'. Despite the Mary Shelley trappings, there seems a genuine commitment beneath; the last line quoted describes the excited speculation and questing of the poem's subject. Such a state of excitement was known to many of Emily's predecessors such as Coleridge, Shelley and Cowper, even if we omit Blake whose poems and engravings Emily could not have seen, though she may have known of him as an artist through Mrs Hemans' poem in *Blackwood's*.[8] The spurious exaggeration of the prisoner's reaction does not quite obscure the reality of his or her haunted mental activity.

After the first four stanzas Emily Brontë reaches a point of calm. Her prisoner has reached 'my own world, my spirit's home', a peaceful region of sea and 'glorious dome'. Though the poem now runs through more stanzas attempting in a rather low key to particularise the

terrifying experience, many of these succeeding lines are failures and
do not touch the inward meaning. However, we may take the poem as a
(very imperfect) account of an inner struggle through intellectual and
even physical turmoil to spiritual calm.

H29, written on 14 October of the same year, deals with a Gondalised experience in which a dreamer hears wailing at night. The
dramatic explanation is that a survivor from battle is moaning nearby
(though not before yew-tree boughs near the shattered window have
been suggested as a possible rational explanation of the sound). Next
month 'A. G. A.' is writing of sleep in a poem beginning 'Sleep brings
no joy to me'.[9] The poem is by no means negligible; for our present
purpose it is valuable to note the second stanza:

> Sleep brings no rest to me;
> The shadows of the dead
> My waking eyes may never see
> Surround my bed.

Emily is now interpreting the nocturnal experience in terms of ghostly
spirits, perhaps under two main influences. The first is the Gothic
tradition, in which nocturnal visions are to be explained (not without
some sensationalism) as revenants. The second is perhaps her own
early loss of her mother and two elder sisters. I have elsewhere
expressed reservations about Winifred Gerin's view that the loss of
Maria was not as crucial to Emily as to Branwell.[10] Even though the
orthodox view of Carus Wilson and others that children taken early
from life had been saved from sin may have had influence at the top of
the minds of the remaining Brontë children, it is unlikely that Emily,
with her rejection of orthodoxy, would have felt this adequate, and it
may indeed seem that the preoccupation with 'life after death' per-
meating *Wuthering Heights* has a close connection with the early loss
of a sister whose personality was as intense and ineradicable as Maria's
appears to have been; it sometimes seems as though Maria is the
unacknowledged contributor to almost all the Brontës' works.

Thus by 1837 we have two apparent ingredients in Emily's 'mystic'
vision. We have the experience of feverish dreaming, sometimes
nightmare of the 'incubus' type, resulting in a sudden waking accompanied by an unearthly sound; and we have the notion that the
personality experienced in the dream may be that of a dead associate.
The reality of these visions, though cooled by reflection and transmission to a Gondalised romantic landscape, is so vital as to lead to

exhaustion, but a subsequent feeling of calm is recognised as 'my spirit's home'.

H37, H45 and H50 cannot be dated accurately, though they all predate 1839. In this group the poet or her subject no longer flinches from the experience she will suffer at night, 'Laid alone in the darkened room'.[11] The 'stern power' about to descend on her is no cheerful one. It seems that, if the reading is correct, joy must be 'congealed' by it. Unlike the nightmare of H12 and H15 this vision may be a waking one. The poet first hears a clock strike ('Listen, 'tis just the hour') and it must seem likely that this is the old Haworth church clock. (As mentioned in Chapter 4, this was a predecessor of the present church clock). The 'awful time' may be midnight, or one o'clock. 'Strange sensations' are then experienced, akin presumably to the froth of intellect noted above. Then it is that the visitant, whatever it may be, arrives. Precisely how this visitant is conceptualised is not clear from the poem, in fact it is typical that Emily Brontë recoils from the difficulty of putting the experience into precise words (and thus perhaps either changing or killing it). It is clear that the vision is monitory and controlling ('stern power') in a way that we do not associate with Emily's dead sister. In Jungian psychology the entity might be equated with an 'animus' figure, directing the subject's personality with a firm hand, a figure which must be obeyed and which is both feared and trusted. In this context the moral aspects of Maria's teaching, regretfully rejected by Branwell and in part boldly questioned by Emily, are not lightly to be overlooked.

The fragment beginning 'All hushed and still within the house' (H45) is too short and incomplete for much to be elicited from it, but its rough state in the manuscript does suggest the labour Emily expended to try to express herself honestly. The contrast between a silent house and a watcher within was one she came back to in 'Silent is the House'. In the present poem she seems to be talking about an experience which will not return. At this, she revolts and insists that memory can bring back the vision. 'Memory has power as real as thine', the final line, is the only one which forbids us to think she is talking of a living person on earth: the involuntary vision can be recalled to order through memory. Such a poem might be dismissed as a sub-Wordsworthian gloss, and in fact Anne's poem 'Memory' does appear to have Wordsworthian touches. But the scored and altered manuscript of 'All hushed and still' is evidence of the intense concentration and eager exploration on which Emily was here engaged. The poem breaks off as she finds she cannot make rational sense of her experience.

A short fragment on MS D5, 'O come again' (H50), identifies the vision as a revenant. It has a 'dwelling dank and cold', and is to visit the poet from it. Once again the poem breaks off and we have it as a four-line stanza, reminiscent of a ballad stanza which has floated from its context. We may perhaps recall that traditional ballads, some of which were perhaps sung to Emily by the servants, or known in Irish versions to Mr Brontë, include some ghostly tales. One which seems near in spirit to Emily's poems on death is 'Cold blows the wind',[12] in which a lover waits (fruitlessly in some respects) for the loved one to emerge from the grave and renew their love. But moving as such songs are, they could not provoke on their own the intense interest in visions and ghosts shown by Emily Brontë.

H55, 'It's over now, I've known it all', cannot be dated, and may well be misplaced in Hatfield's chronology. In this three-stanza fragment Emily seems to be about to recall the story of another visitation, a 'fearful vision', which at first we may think to be the nightmare incubus again. The setting however is not bed, the time not midnight. On this occasion the summer sun was sinking over the hills and the poet appears to locate herself 'in the heath' somewhere away from 'human eye'. We may recall the 1837 birthday note which talks of going out 'to make sure if we get into a humour [for writing]'.

As has been mentioned in Chapter 6 there seems some evidence to suggest that at times Emily Brontë identified her nocturnal visitant with the poet Shelley. This hypothesis is of course quite impossible to substantiate, for so cautious and devious a mind as hers recoils from committing the story clearly to paper. But the 'Dream' which is the subject of H86, a non-Gondal poem, may be another facet of the vision which we have traced so far. Here the attempt to bring back the vision fails: memory this time has *not* the power, and the poet is left lamenting, 'Lost vision! ... / Thou canst not shine again'. On 12 January 1839 Emily wrote a poem in which a Gondal subject sees 'a shadowy spirit come' (H95). As already suggested, there may be traces of 'The Ancient Mariner' here. The poem may strike us as more artificial and deliberate than some earlier ones. The vision has become female and seems to have affinity with some aspects of 'The white goddess' of Robert Graves, or the various tutelary female spirits who appear in the works of George Macdonald. Their common source may perhaps be Novalis, though it is not easy to see how Emily might encounter him before going to Belgium.[13]

'Come hither child', dating from 19 July 1839, which appears on MS D3, is full of correction and hesitation as the poet works to express what she wishes. Its subject is the experience of a marvellously musical and poetic child, who is accosted by a Gondal lady and rebuked for her 'power to touch that string so well'. Both the child and the lady might be thought parts of Emily's psyche; the possible significance of the chronological reference 'When I was hardly six years old' has been mentioned in Chapter 4, but it seems straining likelihood to deny the identity of musically talented Emily, the poet, with the child of which she writes. While we need not follow Miss Romer Wilson (whose over-assured interpretation of the poem in *All Alone* may appear academically incautious) all the way with her theory, the poem is certainly worthy of study in considering Emily's attitude to poetic and visionary inspiration.[14] In reply to the accusation, the child tells of a windy night (later changed to 'festal') on which she escaped from a crowd to nurse her own sorrow. The child imagines all sorts of 'forms of fearful gloom' in the room where she has chosen to hide. She prays for death, but just as calm succeeds the dream of horror in earlier poems referred to, so sweetness follows gloom on this occasion. As the child listens, she hears a note of sweet music, connected in her mind with an archangel. This 'seraph-strain' is repeated three times. The child ends her explanation by saying that she is still able to hear the words and tone when 'all alone'.

While the full purport of the poem is probably beyond recapture, it does appear to be significant. In it, Emily may be explaining in a dramatic context and probably for her own benefit (the poem is not recopied in any copy manuscript, and not published in Emily's lifetime) what is the origin of her own supra-rational poetic drive. In this poem, the vision and poetry are one: without the vision there would be no poetic gift or burden. Like the attainment of calm after the nightmare, a harmony is reached after struggle and wildly sad emotions; the harmony comes at the worst possible moment, and it comes as 'God-given', not from within the poet but from without. Once given, it can be recalled:

> But still the words and still the tone
> Swell round my heart when all alone.

The use of the word 'heart' rather than 'mind' suggests the involuntary and irrational nature of the vision, which in this case is not thought of as returning at the beck of memory. One might look for an antecedent for the poem in such works as 'The Prelude', and indeed the crystallisation of understanding on the part of the Brontës must owe something to Wordsworth as well as to Shelley, Coleridge and the other Romantics.

This does not necessarily invalidate the objective reality of the vision, and we have the mature poetry as artefact of the vision, so that it would seem a little perverse to deny its source. It is not easy to see why Emily should write this poem at this particular time, but it does seem to be offering some guarded clue to the feeling present at the start of Emily's encounter with what Robert Graves would presumably call her 'muse'. Emily is thus a typical Romantic in seeing poetry as a compulsive and inspirational matter, and the poet as an instrument, an 'Aeolian harp', through which the poetry can be played.

1839 was an important year for Emily's poetic development. She is following a path later to be followed *mutatis mutandis* by Anne; a development from Gondal towards the poetic exploration of more personal and more humanly relevant matters. The series of A poems, though not yet collected into their comprehensive manuscript, is well under way. On 29 October she is projected into a thoughtful mood by the sound of the autumn wind, and has wandered far away through the agency of the dark night. In this poem (H120) she considers what she calls her 'old feelings' which from the final verse we may take to be feelings of 'love'. These feelings were once 'kind' and 'cherished', but their light has decayed and their wild fancies will no longer suit.

It is impossible to be sure here that Emily is speaking of the poetic vision; she may in part be proposing a discussion of Gondal. The poem may be part of the Shelleyan group, as may others following this year and in 1840. If one finds the case for a kind of Shelleyan possession unproven, one could look for another once living person who may have affected the poet. Such biographical research is likely to be a wild-goose chase, but it does seem clear that some quite specific actual personality is being referred to in these non-Gondal poems.

From 1840 we find in Emily Brontë's poetry increasing evidence of her dedication to a quest we may call philosophical, and her puzzlement at this quest. In May 1841 she addresses rhetorically a 'lonely dreamer' and wonders whether Nature may be able to return the dreamer to peace. The regions in which her mind is moving are 'dark'; her mind's 'roving' is 'useless'. Note that once again Gondal is not involved here. It is not the pull of Gondal that Nature pleads against, but the pull of a ceaseless intellectual search which will not let the poet go. Charlotte, it must be remembered, saw her sister partly as an intellect: 'Ellis will not be seen in his full strength till he is seen as an essayist.'[15] This odd misjudgement gives a clue to Charlotte, whose own mind was busy with ethical considerations and whose feeling for the transcendental, though strong, was more compromising and cir-

cumscribed than her sister's. Yet the comment does suggest a view of
Emily as a calm thinker, dreaming in her later years more steadily and
ratiocinatively than in the early days of nightmare. In July 1841 this
calmer vision produces poems welcoming a platonic rebirth after death
and then seeming to doubt the remoteness and incorporeal nature of
such a rebirth.[16]

Poetic output was interrupted by Emily's sojourn in Belgium, but
thought was not. It seems likely that so far removed from Haworth and
the Yorkshire moors, brought into regular contact with new languages
and new literatures, she was able to crystallise some of her thought,
though it was never destined to satisfy her with clarity. There are
unfortunately very few reports of her reading in Belgium. It seems
possible that she developed a strong taste for German literature, which
she would already have met in translation.[17] She is remembered after
her return to have been studying German, not French, in the intervals
between doing the housework.[18] M. Heger, with whom at first Emily
did not 'draw well', later praised her strong intellect.[19] Musically, she
was regarded so highly that she was given as a tutor the most outstand-
ing musician in Belgium.[20] Her French devoirs are evidence of
strength, but there are problems in interpretation since we do not
know the precise degree of freedom accorded to the writer. What
cannot be done is to dismiss the continental influence on Emily on the
grounds that she was only there nine months and did not use an overtly
continental setting for *Wuthering Heights*. The search for exemplars
for the plot of the novel has perhaps obscured the evidence of
considerable Germanic influence on its quality and tone.

By 1843–4, Emily's reading, whether in German or among English
Romantics, began to provide her with a vocabulary in which to discuss
her visionary experience and to try to make rational sense of her poetic
gift. On 13 April she writes beneath a shining moon of 'Fancy', which is
able to bring her rest and bliss. The power she invoked is stronger than
Coleridge's Fancy, nearer to many Romantics' view of Imagination,
but not wholly identified with it. This power can be invoked, as
memory invoked the vision of 1837–8. The poem is philosophical,
exploring the problems of pain and creation with a depth not previously seen. Her 'roving' mind here certainly shows the strength attributed
to it by M. Heger, and partakes of the foreboding side of Romanticism
in a way reminiscent of the French devoirs. We are not far here from
Tess of the d'Urbervilles' 'blighted star'.

That poetry had become a serious and all-consuming passion we
may guess from the joint efforts in 1843–4 by Emily and Anne to

organise their work into thematically arranged copy-books. This led to the commencement of the two best known of Emily's manuscripts in February 1844. The power addressed as 'My Comforter' in H168 is evidently some aspect of the 'vision' which we have been exploring. One might perhaps suggest that the 'voice' in question is only regarded as a voice through a superficial metaphor; the comfort might perhaps be offered by Shelley or some other non-Christian, whose poems or other writings Emily might be supposed to be reading. Thus the aurally-minded Emily might be 'hearing' what was in fact written on the printed page before her. This may be so, though the attempts to describe the comforter through simile in stanza 6 do not seem quite in accord with such a view:

> Like a soft air above a sea
> Tossed by the tempest's stir –
> A thaw-wind melting quietly
> The snow-drift on some wintery lea.

This does not seem energetic enough to describe the fervour of Shelley, though there are passages of his poetry which might perhaps evoke such a calm response. It is also possible that Emily is referring to poetry in the abstract, yet the anti-Christian reference of stanzas 3 – 5 seems specific. Alternatively, she may be thinking of the philosophy of Shelley (or possibly another poet) not only as expressed in his written work, but also as apparently mediated to her 'savage' heart through an inner interpretative voice of her own. The 'vision' concept is used slightly playfully, not intensely as in the early nightmare poems, but a similar transition from distraught or upsetting feeling to calm is described.

In 'A Day Dream', composed on 5 March 1844, Emily explores the question of transience and eternity through the medium of vision. Unlike many of her poems this one is set in broad daylight and is given a dramatic date, the end of May, different from the time of year in which it was actually written. A dialogue takes place between the poet and her 'heart':

> I took my heart to me
> And we together gladly sank
> Into a reverie.[21]

The poem develops elements both Shelleyan and Coleridgean, but without the commitment of either poet. It is as though the rational part of Emily's mind will not allow her to believe in the 'spirits' she claims to see. This tentative approach to her central theme has the effect of devaluing it, the light rhythm helping to convey a notion of mockery. But we may feel that the poet's withdrawal from involvement does not quite conceal genuine concern for the vision accorded by 'Fancy'. By the time *Wuthering Heights* is reached such a normalising detachment provides a very important element in the novel, but as poetry it is defective in warmth and certainly a long way from the less technically advanced 'dream of horror'.

In a more seriously expressed poem which may comment directly on the foregoing, Emily writes on 3 September 1844 'To Imagination' as a benignant power. She here associates this power with 'a voice divine', which seems one stage nearer to the vision of the early poems. Even here she is tentative and unwilling to place any reliance on the power: 'I trust not to thy phantom bliss'. Within six weeks we have a more forceful statement defying rationalism (which she now calls 'Reason') and erecting Imagination as a sovereign principle. In this sense she may be using the word 'Imagination' ('God of Visions') to include the Gondal narrative, but the scope of her understanding goes far beyond. She speaks of her vision as 'My slave, my comrade and my King', using almost theological language and for the first time bringing under one banner her differing imaginary experiences, of Gondal, which she can alter at will, and of Fancy, which may come to her at night or during daylight, and the unasked vision, 'My Darling Pain that wounds and sears'. The poem is rationally controlled, but reflects the earlier visionary experiences in such lines as 'And wrings a blessing out from tears'.

We come now to the final poetic period, contemporary with *Wuthering Heights*, in which vision comes to be seen as an 'Intimation of Immortality' or as a window from this world to the next. It may well be that Emily Brontë's firmest statements about the nature of this vision occur in the novel rather than in the poems. One may see as one reason for the novel's composition the author's need to explore and try to reconcile disparate elements in her personality and experience. Many of the concerns of the poetry are taken up and deepened in the novel: spirits, dreams and visions are its staple. We may note the violence of the dream attacks suffered both by the supercilious Lockwood and the intense Catherine, echoing Emily's earlier phrase 'My Darling Pain'.

If *Wuthering Heights* can be seen on one level as an attempt by its author to rehearse her own conflicts (tensions which some critics see as resolved by the apparently calm ending), a more explicit statement of the same problems occurs in 'The Philosopher', written on 3 February 1845. Dramatically organised through the use of a detached Nelly-figure, the poem talks of three warring gods, and ends with the wish that the Philosopher may die and thus obtain rest from the continuing laceration. It would surely be perverse to deny that Emily whom M. Heger saw as so intellectually thrusting is represented here by the 'space-sweeping soul' of the philospher. Central to the poem is the philosopher's elusive sight of a 'spirit' which would unite and turn to dazzling beauty the three rivers which circled his feet.

The poem is Emily's clearest statement of the reconciling power of the seraph mentioned intermittently throughout her poetry and whose development we have been tracing. But we receive a severe shock when the philosopher claims never '*Once*' to have seen the spirit's glorious eye light the wildering clouds. Yet in a previous stanza the spirit has been presented as part of a vision of three tumbling rivers which merge in an inky sea, thus echoing distantly the sunless sea of Kubla Khan. There follows the vision of a spirit reconciling three streams:

> Then-kindling all with sudden blaze,
> The glad deep sparkled wide and bright –
> White as the sun; far, far more fair
> Than the divided sources were!

But we are then told in the next two stanzas that the vision conjured up is an unreal one which has never actually been encountered. This is somewhat complex and repeats the withdrawal from her visionary experience which we noted in poems of the previous year with their flippant and scoffing tone. However, we may have grown used to the notion that Emily Brontë's work does not present a coherent organised philosophical viewpoint, but often posits contrasting viewpoints equally strongly. Catherine may well choose Edgar when he is present (and not necessarily for reasons of social advancement as some critics seem to think), but she loves Heathcliff in a different mode when he is in the ascendancy. The image of the three bright streams and their unifying spirit is certainly a real one, even if harshly denied almost immediately.

All the poems of 1845 have a transcendental quality, and there is some evidence of personal as well as poetic equilibrium. Emily's 1845 diary paper, for example, is much more sanguine than Anne's. The June poem 'How beautiful the earth is still' (H188) has an air of serenity and appears to contrast the poet's wise detachment from the world with the emotional devastation of those who were her 'own compeers'.[22] In this poem the 'Glad comforter' seems to be identified with Hope; it was given the title 'Anticipation' in the 1846 printing. But the vision is subdued, not the brilliant integrating spirit of 'The Philosopher', nor the searing apparition of the early work. While Emily Brontë capitalises 'Hope' and personifies the 'thoughtful Spirit' which has taught her the transcendental message, there is no sense here of a vivid encounter with an external power; rather the poem celebrates a calm feeling of unity with nature and with eternity reflected in nature's universality. Nightmare revelation is far away.

The most extraordinary poem of the year, which presents great editorial problems, is that dated 9 October, in which a direct description of the visionary experience is embedded in Gondal narrative, yet seems to protrude from that narrative like a mountain from a desert plain. A full discussion of how this may have happened is inappropriate at the present moment, but the two visionary sections of the poem, stanzas 1–3 and 17–23, cannot be omitted from an account of Emily Brontë's treatment of vision, and have in fact been regarded as her clearest statement of mystical experience.

There must be some difficulty in relating the first few stanzas to the rest of the poem at all. It appears to set the scene: night, silent and snowy, with a 'wanderer', apparently identified with an 'angel' which 'nightly tracks that waste of snow'. The scene thus described is never again referred to, and the nature of the wanderer in no way clarified. The 'I' of the poem, said in the second stanza to be trimming the lamp to guide the wanderer, departs into a Gondal prison, and when the next visionary section opens it is the lady prisoner in the dungeon who gives her personal account of supernatural visitation. There has presumably been some kind of a break in Emily's rational organisation of the poem, but an emotional link is present, and for all the wavering incongruity of the story as presented, the material of stanzas 17–23 does not seem alien to that of the first three stanzas.

Once the prisoner 'A. G. Rochelle', who may possibly be the same as 'A. G. A.' of earlier poems, begins to relate her experience, her narrative is specific and gripping. She starts with a reference to 'western winds', which may remind us once more of Shelley. As the night becomes clearer, 'visions rise and change which kill me with desire'; this is the kind of πόθος which includes Wordsworth's groping for a recall of life before birth, as well as the desire of 'The Philosopher' for a reconciling spirit, and the intense yearning of Catherine and Heathcliff in *Wuthering Heights*. She appears to be about to specify it, but can only do so by negatives, by denying that it has to do with the warm flashes generated by 'sun or thunderstorm'. She approaches the core of her meaning so nearly as to suggest that this feeling was best known in infancy, and we remember the seraph's strain of 'Come hither, child'. The intensity of stanza 19 with its 'when joy grew mad with awe at counting future tears' is quite remarkable, helped poetically as it is by the stark monosyllables. Despite the negative form of this stanza, we feel that the poet is referring to a vision fitfully pursued even in adult life.

There follows a struggle which is described in sharply physical terms; one is reminded of descriptions of mediumistic possession, from Virgil's Sybil in *Aeneid* Book VI onward. The Sybil is shown to be in physical anguish, trying to 'throw off' the god from her breast, and Emily Brontë writes, 'The more that anguish racks the earlier it will bless'. 'Mute music' succeeds the struggle, just as the Sybil's raving words and her 'fury' are succeeded by quiet.[23] The exact order of events in Emily's description of 'mystic' possession is unclear, and we are left in some doubt about the nature of the central revelation. It does, however, strongly recall those earlier accounts of nightmare succeeded by calm which the poet had written eight years previously. We have reached 'my spirit's home'.

It would seem that we can discern a consistent vein throughout Emily Brontë's poetry, which is again present in *Wuthering Heights*. External biographical evidence is lacking, but the central experience is described in the poems so forcefully and so consistently (it often inspires passages which stand out as genuine in the midst of Gondal flounderings) that most interpreters of her poems, whether popular or scholarly, appear to consent to the notion that she is putting a personal experience into the mouths of these Gondal characters and using her poetry in part to explore the nature of her gift or bane. Again and again throughout her life she approaches the subject of vision, tentatively and fitfully, ready to be distracted or diverted, and apt to fritter away her opportunities in Gondal pseudo-drama. We never obtain from this 'taciturn' writer a full statement of belief or a clinical analysis of the transcendent dream, so that a considerable part of her poetry may strike one as unfulfilled gropings towards a revelation. *Wuthering Heights* appears to have been necessary for the full account to be rendered. Here too, we are in a poetic world, a world of myth and metaphor, in which the author discusses all her major interests in a wider context than she is able to do within the confines of lyric, or even lengthy narrative verse.

It seems a fair hypothesis that the original and probably recurring experience must have been a puzzling and powerful encounter with what appeared as an external force within the dream world. This event could well have been what Jungian psychologists attribute to a meeting with an archetypal figure, perhaps the 'animus'; so startling a 'dream of horror' would be of searing effect in the case of such a sensitive personality as Emily Brontë's.

One may perhaps be inclined to ascribe the beginning of these visions to the deprivation of Maria, the substitute mother. In an interesting article in *New Society* in 1980 John Bowlby shows how bereaved children may see visions of their lost parents, and instances the case of a six-year-old girl who, 'Before getting up in the morning ... frequently had the experience of seeing her mother sitting on her bed talking quietly to her, much as she had when she was alive'.[24] If Emily Brontë had encountered such a dream, perhaps recurrently, she may well have felt compelled to ponder its meaning and interpret for herself its importance.

Human experience naturally takes on a subjective colouring, and will be interpreted in terms of the theories current at the time and the notions held and rationally comprehended by the mind of the subject. Once the interpretation has begun, the experiences themselves will start to be shaped by that very interpretation. Thus Emily Brontë, overpowered at night by a demonic entity, seeks explanation for this among the Romantic poets she knows, and among Gothic novel writers. As her understanding proceeds, she sees her experience in the light of Coleridge, Shelley and Wordsworth, and this vision once cautiously adopted, produces more experiences of the type diagnosed by Emily's conscious mind.

In other civilisations at other times, Emily might have seen herself as a Sybil, or felt called to be a nun with a personal vision of God (at times this was not far from the explanation proposed for herself by the more orthodox Anne); in the twentieth century she might have supposed she had some psychological problem and must consult a psychiatrist. It seems clear from biographical hints that she thought herself sufficiently unlike her fellows as to be always on guard against their ridicule. When Charlotte urged publication, a procedure with which the Brontës' minds had often played, Emily's objections would have to do with the reluctance to be in print and still be unable to communicate, so that her isolation would become irrevocable; there are indeed suggestions that the adverse reception of *Wuthering Heights* affected her in exactly this way.[25]

Meanwhile we note several phases in the development of Emily's understanding and descriptions of the dream experience. At first there is intensity of dislike; then there is the calm which follows fear and leads to 'my spirit's home'. The move here towards Shelleyan pantheism is perfectly natural given the traditional doctrines of heaven in which the Brontës grew up. The emphasis in traditional, including evangelical, Christianity on life in another, better world was still a commonplace, and when such a better world was regarded as a certainty (with the terrifying alternative future of hell almost equally so), the approach to it through Shelleyan pantheism could appear to Emily Brontë as only a variant of philosophical emphasis.

From the first, the dream experience is conceived to be connected with poetic inspiration, which is sometimes gladly acknowledged in Emily's poems and sometimes sought unavailingly. Her theology is from the chief Romantics, who see in their various ways poetry descending platonically from heaven. They are of course in a classical as well as a Biblical and folk tradition, equating poet with prophet, a role which Emily does not feel fitted to undertake, though in *Wuthering Heights* she espouses the part of educator to Lockwood. We have seen that there is a questing and doubting note even in her later 'inspired' verse, and it seems a complete interpretation is still eluding her. The scoffing tone of 'On a sunny brae' shows the poet unable to abandon herself to the vision, hardened as she is by the buffets of daily life. She shares here one of her sister Anne's major preoccupations, the hardening effect of time, chilling youth's genuineness and ardour, and the theme is also found in Branwell's poems. Though the Brontës do not adopt Wordsworth's explanation *in toto*, the influence is clear.

There is also the strange attempt to interpret the dream experience as the vision of a young companion, visiting the poet at night just as Heathcliff thought Catherine was trying to visit him at night in the 'oak closet' scene. While she felt it possible to interpret the dream in this way, Emily appears to have been able to maintain some kind of ideal relationship, possibly with Shelley, the nature of which sounds quite ridiculous to twentieth-century ears. The whole tone of *Wuthering Heights*, with its repeated notion of communion external to the physical body, taking place between the living and the dead, gives rise to the feeling that its author gave her emotional assent to the possibility of such an association.

However she explained it, this experience seems to have recurred at least until 1845, and to have continued to sear her. The poem 'Silent is the House' is so imperfect that it gives no real clue to the nature of the nocturnal visitant and even seems to confuse the two main actors in its narrative (dare one say that Emily Brontë did not really care if it appeared that 'Julian' and 'A. G. Rochelle' *were* each other?). However, no one can read it without the feeling that for the poet this was a vital preoccupation, which had to be dealt with. Whether this recurrent dream and vision, followed by periods of thought in which the vision's purport had to be mulled over, can be described as 'mysticism' is an open question. The sense of communion with something outside the poet is strong; but the precise nature of the divinity inherent in the 'something' is plainly as obscure to the poet as to her readers. Whereas Anne Brontë talked to her God, or her Saviour, in a manner quite acceptable to the evangelicals, Emily used no such names: the signs are that she shares Shelley's hatred of them and in particular refuses to accept a Christian notion of 'sin'. Nevertheless it would be quite wrong to suggest that her religious quest is totally unorthodox or totally without guidance.

'I'll walk where my own nature would be leading', she writes. But the pathway leads through land opened up by Plato and his successors, and recently re-explored by Wordsworth, Coleridge and Shelley. It is in this light, rather than in the 'glare of hell' that we need to look at the content of Emily Brontë's inspirational output.

NOTES

1. D. P. Drew, 'Emily Brontë and Emily Dickinson as Mystic Poets', *BST*, vol. LXXVIII (1968) pp. 227–32.
2. See Chapters 4 and 5.
3. As previously, Hatfield's MS classification is used.
4. Shackleton's weather records, at Cliffe Castle, Keighley.
5. It is possible that H13, immediately following this, should be printed as part of the same poem.
6. Ann Faraday, *The Dream Game* (London, 1976) p. 199.
7. H15, lines 1–2.
8. *Blackwood's Magazine*, vol. XXXI (February 1832) pp. 220–1.
9. H34.
10. See Chapter 4, and W. Gerin, *Emily Brontë* (Oxford, 1971) p. 9.
11. H37, line 2.
12. F. Child, *The English and Scottish Popular Ballads* (New York, 1890) vol. IV, p. 474. See also A. Smith (ed.), *The Art of Emily Brontë* (London, 1976) pp. 172–5.
13. The parallels between Emily Brontë and Novalis deserve study. Novalis' crucial separation was from his bride, Sophie. Among works of his which Emily would find intensely interesting are *Hymnen an die Nacht*. If she

made acquaintance with these and other Romantic works while in
Belgium, this might provide the motivation for learning German in
Haworth parsonage kitchen.

14. R. Wilson, *All Alone* (London, 1928) facing p. 172, etc.
15. Letter from Charlotte Brontë to W. S. Williams, 15 February 1848.
16. H148 and H149.
17. For example, in *Blackwood's* – see Gerin, *Emily Brontë*, p. 217.
18. E. Gaskell, *The Life of Charlotte Brontë* (London, 1857) Chapter 8.
19. Ibid., Chapter 11.
20. Gerin, *Emily Brontë*, p. 133.
21. H170, lines 22–4.
22. H188, lines 11ff.
23. Virgil, *Aeneid*, Book VI, pp. 77ff.
24. J. Bowlby, 'How Will Mummy Breathe and Who Will Feed Her?', *New Society*, 6 March 1980, pp. 492ff.
25. For this period in her life and her reactions to publication, see Gerin, *Emily Brontë*, Chapter 16.

11 Ellen Nussey and the Brontës

TOM WINNIFRITH

Generations of Brontë students have owed an immense debt of gratitude to Ellen Nussey for preserving Charlotte Brontë's letters to her, thus providing an indispensable chronological framework for subsequent biographers. In *The Brontës and their Background*[1] I tried to show how Ellen's efforts to publish the letters ended tragically in the 1890s with both the letters themselves and the permission to publish them in the hands of the incompetent and dishonest C. K. Shorter and T. J. Wise. Ellen Nussey's own letters at this time make pathetic reading, and we cannot help feeling a great deal of sympathy for her.

In the Berg Collection, New York, there are documents which perhaps remove some of this sympathy, although at the same time shedding a great deal of light on the Brontë story.[2] These documents consist of sixteen pages in Ellen Nussey's handwriting about the Brontës, twelve letters from Ellen Nussey to T. Wemyss Reid, and one letter from Nicholls to Reid, who was the author of the second Brontë biography. The sixteen pages were used by Reid in his biography,[3] and the letters show how this biography came about, while at the same time making many additional remarks about various members of the Brontë family.

One of the irritating things about the letters to Reid is Ellen's claim that his book was bound to be more valuable than Mrs Gaskell's life, although posterity has hardly agreed. Reid, though he printed a few additional letters and recorded a few additional incidents, hardly added much to our knowledge of the Brontës. One reason for this is Ellen's morbid anxiety to avoid giving offence to anybody. Thus we find, for instance, her objecting to her brother Henry being named even by the letter H on the grounds that Henry's wife was still alive and might be offended by Henry's proposal to Charlotte, although actually she ought to have been flattered. Another reason is her wish to present

128

Charlotte as someone with a totally unsullied reputation, a worthy wish that could lend itself to distortions. She objected to the emphasis Mrs Gaskell had put on Branwell. It is possible that Mrs Gaskell exaggerates and antedates Branwell's troubles as a smokescreen to hide Charlotte's troubles with M. Heger, but this of course is not the reason why Ellen objected to the part Branwell was made to play by Mrs Gaskell. She says on 6 November 1876 that 'it is a very bad injustice to her memory that one so pure and excellent as she was should have any word connected with her printed life that is unsuited to the reading of the young and innocent'.

The sixteen-page narrative was clearly used as material by Wemyss Reid, since from it he derived the story of the visit to Bolton Abbey in 1838. Interestingly, Ellen Nussey's account is not the same as Reid's for this incident. In Reid's account some emphasis is laid on the shabbiness of the Brontë party and the shame they felt, and in Miss Gerin's life of Branwell Brontë the episode is seen as an important stage in his humiliating inability to get on in the world.[4] Reading between the lines of Ellen's patronising account it is possible that both Reid and Miss Gerin are right in stressing the shame and humiliation which the Brontës felt, but Ellen does not actually say this. She says that the Brontë gig was shabby, but that it was cordially received by the coach and pair arrivals. Ellen admired Branwell's brilliance and his quotations of poetry, but saw the dangers ahead of him. Branwell's appearance was grotesque as none of the Brontës understood dress until Charlotte and Emily had been to Brussels. The conclusion of the account of the Brontës' visit to Bolton Abbey reads rather nauseatingly, 'They left friends (whose route lay in another direction) full of grateful pleasure and happiness for the day's enjoyment which had proved to all a treat greater than had been anticipated.'

Before this account Ellen, whose narrative is organised in a haphazard fashion, discusses the Brontës as Sunday-school teachers. Anne and Charlotte were faithful in this office. Once a year they invited their pupils up to the parsonage. The pupils were rough and genial, but Emily said it was a vain attempt to try and teach them good manners. The Brontës were eager to play games with their charges, but did not know how to do so. Emily's recorded remarks are so few that we are grateful for this curt comment, but in general we feel that this passage shows the Brontës' inability to get on with their supposed social inferiors, and indeed, whether consciously or unconsciously, Ellen's narrative does seem to stress the Brontës' isolation.[5]

At about this time, she says, and she is presumably talking of 1838, the year of the Bolton Abbey expedition, Charlotte was very busy painting, spending nine hours with scarcely an interval at her work. Anne and Emily were also busy with their pencils, but chiefly as a recreation or to teach others should the need arise. There are shades of *Agnes Grey* here, a novel which with the Grey family cut off by their rich relatives and cut off from their neighbours echoes most clearly the Brontës' isolation.

The next topic discussed by Ellen is surprising, as it sheds an unexpectedly favourable light on Mr Brontë, who elsewhere in this account, and Wemyss Reid's monograph and especially in Ellen's letters to Reid, is not at all favourably treated. Mr Brontë is said to have frequently made efforts to improve the sanitary conditions of the village, but in spite of his efforts the passing bell was often a dreary accompaniment to the day's engagements. Indeed Ellen like every other visitor to Haworth saw what a sombre effect the churchyard must have had. Surprisingly, however, the inhabitants of Haworth did not seem to find the churchyard gloomy, since they used it for drying their washing. Mr Brontë, presumably worried by spiritual as well as sanitary considerations, put a stop to this practice, and even wrote some bad verses on the subject which conclude:

> The females all would have fled with their clothes
> To stockyards and backyards, where noone knows,
> And loudly have sworn by the suds which they swim in
> They'll wring off his head for his warring with women,
> While their husbands combine and roar out in their fury
> They'll lynch him at once without trial by jury,
> But saddest of all the fair maidens declare
> Of marriage or love he must ever despair.

One cannot admire Mr Brontë's tact any more than his verse, but one can praise his courage, especially perhaps the wry reference to his status as a widower in the final two lines.

In the next and final paragraph Mr Brontë appears in a less good light. After leaving school the Brontës were buoyant and happy, but there then followed a long period of gloom due to their unsuitability as governesses: 'Had Mr Brontë lived more in his family circle and turned his knowledge of human nature on his own children, he surely would have influenced them to have chosen any vocation other than that of governess'. Ellen is surely unjust here, as there is no evidence of Mr Brontë bringing any pressure on his daughters, nor is it easy to see what alternative profession the girls could have adopted. Ellen ends her narrative by saying that at home the sisters were the bravest of the brave, but 'Charlotte had a painful conviction that living in other people's houses was to all of them an estrangement from their real characters. It compelled them to adopt an exterior which was a bona fide suppression, an alienation from themselves, and they suffered accordingly.'

So much for the consecutive narrative. The letters are naturally even less coherent, and many of them are taken up with complaints about the Post Office or about Ellen Nussey's health. Wemyss Reid, whose letters in reply can be found in the last volume of the Shakespeare Head edition,[6] appears to have been remarkably patient. Ellen was about sixty at the time of the letters, written between 1876 and 1878, but she appears to vary between the querulousness of old age and childish jealousy. We have already shown how she is contemptuous of Mrs Gaskell; to this she now adds some very rude remarks about Mr Nicholls and Mr Brontë, under whose aegis of course Mrs Gaskell had produced her biography. Nevertheless Ellen's letters to Reid do contain important new information about the Brontës, although given her state of mind we should not regard this information as totally reliable.

In a letter of 4 July 1876 she complains she has already been the victim of small talk, and endured the malice and narrowness of local gossip. It is difficult to see why. She also exaggerates the splendour of her family's social position when she talks of Rydings, an old turretted house in which many generations of their family had lived, and which remained their property even when Ellen removed to Brookroyd. This picture has been generally accepted by biographers, but is not really true.[7]

On 7 July 1876 Ellen expresses some nervousness on reading the proofs that Reid had made matters too plain, but says that these had died away on a second reading. She adds inconsequentially that Mr Sowden, a clerical friend of Mr Nicholls, had fits and had died after falling into the river. She is glad that her friend is so nobly depicted, and adds sententiously that if we had more women like Charlotte Brontë how much better the world would be. In a later letter, undated, but evidently written shortly after this, she repeats her praise of Reid's book, and says that she would think Mr Nicholls would bite his nails, but that he had better stop there, as Currer Bell was none of his. Mr Nicholls is advised rather oddly to read the life of the Prince Consort, and Ellen ends piously with the reflection that the pure and upright have nothing to fear except the last judgement.

Mr Nicholls's reaction was slow in coming, but savage when it came. The letter in the Berg Collection dated 6 November 1876 is not the first letter of complaint, but is said by Wemyss Reid to be much milder than the original one which must have been written at the end of October. Ellen Nussey says on 3 November that the peremptory letter from Mr Nicholls did not surprise her, as he was always pugnaciously inclined, and Charlotte used to say that he enjoyed whacking the boys in schools. She says, although the savage nature of her letter makes this doubtful, that she is obliged that Mr Nicholls had shown his hand, and recommends that Lord Houghton should try to control him.

After this she turns to a general attack on Mr Nicholls and Mr Brontë. Mr Nicholls is described as 'far too pig-headed and obtuse to be mated with a being like Charlotte – but for his selfishness and want of perception I believe Charlotte would have been alive now'. This is presumably a reference to Charlotte's fatal walk across the moors rather than to her alleged pregnancy. But Mr Brontë receives even shorter shrift, and Ellen puts the blame on him for the enmity of Mr Nicholls: 'There is no knowing what villainies old Mr Brontë had put in his head.' Wemyss Reid had better know the worst of 'the old villain'. Mary Taylor's remark about 'that wicked old man' is quoted. Ellen says: 'the consummate vanity of the man made him equal to any artifice for revenge. He did his best to alienate Charlotte's faithful heart from her faithful friend even when I was in the house the last visit before the marriage. She turned upon him with rage as we breakfasted when he made some kind of hypocritical remark to me on the vicissitudes of life.'

Ellen says this cannot be alluded to, but oddly enough Wemyss Reid does give a hostile portrait of Mr Brontë, and even mentions the incident at the breakfast table, not that this has played a very prominent part in various portraits of Charlotte as a dutiful daughter. Ellen was clearly in a bad mood when she wrote this letter, presumably being upset by Mr Nicholls's attack. She ends her letter with a vitriolic attack on the wife of Matthew Taylor, who married beneath him, a woman 'stuck up, narrow and vulgar, but yet one of those women who acquire great influence, especially with your sex'. So it is not just Mr Nicholls and Mr Brontë who feel Ellen's wrath. And yet the attacks on Charlotte's father and husband are so violent as to be almost inexplicable.

Mr Nicholls's letter of 6 November to Wemyss Reid is a dignified contrast. He is pleased by the general portrait of his wife, although he did not like the reference to Mr Taylor, one of Charlotte's suitors, nor the hostility to Mr Brontë, who, although he had his peculiarities, and opposed the marriage, was revered by Mr Nicholls as one of the best and truest friends he ever had. He is, however, very angry with Ellen Nussey. Had he known other letters existed other than those passed to Mrs Gaskell he would have asked Ellen Nussey to destroy them, as he had already asked Miss Wooler who had anticipated his wishes. He should have warned Ellen, but did not think 'she would be so unmindful of what was due to the memory of the dead and the feeling of the living'.

Mr Nicholls's tone is dignified, but his desire to suppress the surviving letters of Charlotte seems neither reasonable, nor helpful to students of the Brontës. We see in the Berg Collection the fatal quarrel between Mr Nicholls and Ellen Nussey which was to play into the hands of Wise and Shorter. It is difficult to see why both parties adopted such entrenched attitudes. Clearly both sides were jealous of the way in which Charlotte had loved the other, and both thought that they should be in control of the writing of the life, but given the fact that Charlotte in her way had loved both, and that both shared the material for any biography, with Ellen owning the letters and Mr Nicholls the copyright, one would have thought some compromise possible.

It is possible that one reason for Mr Nicholls's anxiety is his fear that Ellen might have letters revealing Charlotte's love for M. Heger. It is of course a fascinating question, not unfortunately possible to answer with any certainty, just how far the various parties connected with Charlotte's biography knew of her love for M. Heger. Mrs Gaskell certainly knew of this; she visited M. Heger in Belgium, there are various nervous references in her correspondence to the perils resulting from the publication of *The Professor*, and quite probably Charlotte finding a sympathetic ear in her loneliness as she wrote *Villette* told all to Mrs Gaskell. Mr Nicholls probably knew something, as Charlotte would have felt obliged to tell him something, and after all her revelations were hardly as lurid as those of Tolstoy or Tess of the d'Urbervilles.

Ellen Nussey probably knew very little. The letters to Ellen Nussey that survive are remarkably circumspect about M. Heger, and if Ellen destroyed some more revealing correspondence, her hypocrisy in stressing Charlotte's purity was considerable. Of course it is difficult for us now to penetrate the primness of Victorian middle class society, but Ellen's letters to Wemyss Reid are a monument to this primness, which Charlotte would not have wished to shock. Charlotte was of course remarkably reluctant to reveal to Ellen her authorship of *Jane Eyre*. It might be argued that Ellen would have to have been strangely unperceptive not to have known about her friend's unlucky passion, but the letters in the Berg Collection do not seem very perceptive. Reid presumably knew nothing of M. Heger; he says jovially that some people thought that Charlotte had lost her heart in Brussels, but that this was not true.

Ellen's anxiety to protect Charlotte's moral reputation is shown when she tries in a letter of 20 November to answer the charge of Harriet Martineau that Charlotte made her heroines fall in love first. On the contrary says Ellen, there is a peculiar charm in Charlotte's delineation of love in that the attraction of hero and heroine is mutual. It is not the case that Charlotte's heroines make up to the heroes, and she hopes that Reid will be able to point this out.

In the same letter Ellen refers to the portrait of Cowan Bridge as Lowood, and says that this was essentially a just portrait. She then confuses the issue by saying that the identity of Lowood and Cowan Bridge was supported by Miss Evans, the original of Miss Temple, sister of Dr Evans, the head of a college in the United States. There has been some confusion over the identity of the real Miss Temple, but most of our sources say she was the wife of Dr Evans: they also tend to play down the support she gave to the portrait of Lowood.[8]

On 24 November Ellen says there is no portrait of Charlotte Brontë except that by Richmond. She said there had been a painting in oils by Branwell of Emily, Anne and Branwell (and presumably of Charlotte too, although Ellen does not say this), but as well as being a very bad portrait it was also a very bad likeness. So much for the Pillar portrait, to which Ellen is presumably referring; the sisters do look remarkably plain in this painting.

In the same letter Ellen makes some very interesting remarks about *Wuthering Heights*. She says she has only read the novel once, and clearly disapproves of it. She felt very certain that Emily had taken her characters from the dreadfully weird life-stories that Mr Brontë used to tell with great gusto of some of the old inhabitants in out of the way places over the moors. 'I used to shudder at his recitals and I can see his eyes now as they gleamed at my (I am sure) blanched look, for I was frightened in my innocence and ignorance of such beings as he described. These stories were always given in early days as we sat around the breakfast and tea table when Miss Branwell presided. I understood, though I tried to hear as little as I could, that he was relating what others had told him.'

Wemyss Reid does take up this reference in his account of *Wuthering Heights*, but there broadens the account of the sources to include Ireland as well. Ellen's account would seem to favour Yorkshire, rather than Ireland, or German romantic tales as the source of Emily's inspiration, although her blanched face and closed ears do not make her a very reliable informant. We must make some allowance for her wish, perhaps unconscious, to discredit Mr Brontë by associating him with *Wuthering Heights*, and vice versa. In actual fact Mr Brontë emerges from Ellen's account as a rather less distant figure than he appears in some Brontë biographies, and, if he is partly responsible for the origins of *Wuthering Heights*, then our debt to him is immense.

Reid's articles were expanded into a book in 1877, and Ellen's subsequent letters are less interesting. On 10 May 1877 she says that it is a good idea that the letters should be consigned eventually to the British Museum, and she mentions this again in a letter of 2 February 1878. On 20 November she is angry with Mrs Firth for suggesting that the Brontës had £400 a year. Miss Branwell had only a life annuity, and this was probably one reason why Mr Brontë turned a cold shoulder on any Branwell relatives. The logic of this remark is not clear. Nor is it quite clear what Ellen means by making an attack, which she says Charlotte would have appreciated, on Miss Wooler for demanding money for letters. It is odd that Mr Nicholls thought that Miss Wooler had destroyed Charlotte's letters to her as evidently she did not, although she may have destroyed some referring to Mr Nicholls.

There is one undated letter which appears in the order in which the letters are collected to be dated 23 January 1878, but the year looks more like 1873, and since in this letter Ellen offers Reid letters it would seem to antedate the whole of Reid's work. In it Ellen says that Mrs Gaskell originally intended her biography to be only one volume, but that Smith had persuaded her to extend this to two. This innocent expansion by Mrs Gaskell is just one of many grievances that Ellen Nussey mentions in some correspondence from the declining years of her life.

Not all this correspondence has yet been made available, and in *The Brontës and their Background* I had to make guesses about exactly what had happened. There are about a dozen letters in the Humanities Research Center, Texas. Some of these letters are duplicates of letters in England; it is interesting that Ellen made three copies of a letter to Wise dated 26 July 1895, saying that she had sold him letters for £125 to be deposited in the British Museum, of which two are at Texas, and there are also two copies in Texas of a memorandum to the effect that she had left letters to J. Horsfall Turner in 1887 on the understanding that these were not to be published until after her death. It is difficult to see how the story of the defrauding of Ellen Nussey can be kept secret with so many copies about.

The Texas letters do throw up incidental remarks about the Brontë story as well as the Ellen Nussey story, although Ellen's embittered state must make us sceptical about some of these. On 24 September 1883 she writes to Mary Robinson, the author of the first biography of Emily Brontë, about Leyland's book on Branwell. Leyland she says is wrong to blame the Brontë sisters or Ellen herself for giving such a bad account of Branwell to Mrs Gaskell. Ellen had only given permission for extracts from her correspondence to be used in what was originally intended to be a lengthy article, but had been expanded into two volumes through Smith, Elder & Co.'s desire for commercial gain.

In an unfinished letter to C. K. Shorter of April 1895 Ellen expresses her anger that he should not have an hour to spare to see her, when he had been to see Mr Nicholls who had got hold of all the Brontë money and had not been able or willing to nurse Charlotte Brontë properly. This letter makes painful reading, and it is all the more painful to realise that even as she wrote Shorter had succeeded, where Ellen herself had failed, in persuading Mr Nicholls whether by trickery or bribery, to allow him permission to print unpublished material. It is doubtful how far Shorter's claim to own the copyright of all unpublished Brontë material would stand up to close examination, but he must deserve a certain amount of credit for the way he succeeded in winning over separately both Ellen Nussey and Mr Nicholls.

Had Mr Nicholls and Ellen Nussey had their way, the letters would have been destroyed, and we would have had to derive our knowledge of Charlotte Brontë from Ellen's prim and pallid paraphrases. This is obvious from an undated letter, presumably a copy, which Ellen wrote to Mr Nicholls. The letter which is with the Ellen Nussey letters in the Humanities Research Center Collection, Texas, adds a sad postscript to the whole sorry affair.

Mr dear Mr Nicholls

As you seem to hold in great honor the ardentia verba of feminine epistles I pledge myself to the destruction of Charlotte's epistles, henceforth, if you pledge yourself to no censorship in the matter communicated.

Yours very truly E. Nussey

To this Ellen has added a note in pencil, 'Mr N. continued his censorship, so the pledge was void'.

One must be glad that the pledge was void. Even imperfectly edited, and still containing some of Ellen's own bowdlerisations and unreliable dates, Charlotte Brontë's letters to Ellen Nussey are of vital importance. It is true that Ellen, both on the internal evidence of the letters themselves and such external evidence as that provided by the Berg correspondence, does not seem a correspondent likely to provoke very interesting letters. Indeed on reading the letters in the Berg Collection and in the Texas Library we are paradoxically surprised that Charlotte Brontë had any friends at all, and that Ellen Nussey of all people was her friend.

NOTES

1. T. Winnifrith, *The Brontës and their Background* (London, 1973) pp. 195–201.
2. I am grateful to the curators of the Berg Collection for permission to quote from these documents.
3. T. W. Reid, *Charlotte Brontë: A Monograph* (London, 1877).
4. W. Gerin, *Branwell Brontë* (London, 1961) pp. 60–2.
5. This counters the suggestions made by B. and G. Lloyd Evans, *A Companion to the Brontës* (London, 1982), that the Brontës were not isolated, and that Emily made friends easily.
6. *SHBL*, vol. IV, pp. 261–4.
7. Winnifrith, *The Brontës and their Background*, pp. 151–2.
8. B. Harrison, 'The Real Miss Temple', in *BST*, vol. LXXXV (1975) pp. 361–4.

Index

Smith, George, 11, 14, 18, 86, 90, 136
Spark, Muriel, 48, 57, 61, 94, 108
Special Collections Centre, University of Vancouver, viii, 14–18
Stanford, Derek, 41, 48, 53, 57, 61, 108
Swift, Jonathan, 67, 82, 107
Symington, J. A., xii, 15, 17–19, 21

Taylor, Mary, 26, 132
Tenant of Wildfell Hall, The, 62, 85, 87, 91, 92, 94, 99–109
  characters in:
  Arthur the younger, 104
  Halford, 100
  Hargrave, 100, 103
  Hattersley, 100
  Helen, 88, 100, 103–6, 108
  Huntingdon (Arthur), 100, 101, 103, 106–8
  Lawrence, 102
  Lowborough, Lady, 101
  Markham, Gilbert, 99, 102, 103, 107
  preface to, 99, 102, 106, 107
Thorp Green, 92, 97
Thrushcross Grange, 20, 78
Tolkien, J. R. R., 56, 57

Villette, 10, 11, 85, 88, 133
Virgil, 81–2, 123, 127
Visick, Mary, 51, 57

Watkinson, Mrs, of Halifax, 23, 24
Watts, Isaac, 67, 82
Weightman, William, 22, 31, 105

Wesley, John, 63, 67
Wildfell Hall, see Tenant of Wildfell Hall, The
Williams, W. S., 9, 84
Wilson, Rev. Carus, 113
Wilson, Romer, 16, 28, 60, 116, 127
Wise, Thomas, xii, 14–19, 21, 35, 128, 133
Wooler, Eliza, 26, 27
Wooler, Margaret, 22, 23, 25–7, 32, 96, 133, 135
Wordsworth, William, 77–8, 81
Wuthering Heights, xiii, 20, 23, 45, 51, 56, 61, 62, 64, 70, 72, 75, 76, 78, 84–90, 91, 92, 98, 99–104, 106–9, 111, 113, 118, 120, 122–5, 134, 135
  characters in:
  Branderham, Jabez (or Jabes), 107
  Catherine the elder, 56, 61, 62, 64, 88, 90, 103, 104, 106, 120–2, 125
  Catherine the younger, 56, 90, 92
  Edgar Linton, 56, 62, 89, 92, 100, 103, 104, 121
  Hareton, 78, 90, 100
  Heathcliff, xi, 56, 61, 64, 73, 78, 88–90, 94, 95, 100–4, 106, 107, 121, 122, 125
  Hindley, 88–9, 100–2
  Isabella, 88–9
  Joseph, 101
  Linton Heathcliff, 56, 89–90
  Lockwood, 88–9, 100, 107, 111, 120, 121, 125
  Nelly, 62, 88–9, 107

Zamorna, 11, 17